# Murder

# In

# Humboldt

This is the story of a small West Tennessee town turned upside down by labor problems and underworld crime. Then, the murder of a local business figure, which seemed to be connected to both.

## A Carson Reno Mystery

Written by

Gerald W. Darnell

# Murder in Humboldt

Copyright © 2011 by Gerald W. Darnell

ISBN: 978-0-557-73416-0

Second Edition

Gerald W. Darnell

carsonreno@msn.com

**Be sure to check out Carson Reno's other Mystery Adventures**

-------------------------------------------------------------------

*The Price of Beauty in Strawberry Land*

# Killer Among Us

# SUnset 4

# *Horse Tales*

# *the* Crossing

**"Life is cheap – make sure you buy enough"**

*Carson Reno*

# Dedication

To all my friends in Humboldt and
especially HHS classes 62,63,64,65,66 and 67.

# Contribution Credits

Elizabeth Tillman White

Mary Ann Sizer Fisher

# Material Credits

Humboldt Public Library

Gibson County Historical Website

# Murder in Humboldt

## Prologue

The year is 1962 and this small west Tennessee town has been turned upside down by a labor strike at its main manufacturing plant – Wayne Knitting. It seems that, as a result of the strike, some very serious underworld crime problems have surfaced in Humboldt. A small town sheriff and small town Chief of Police have their hands full dealing with the strike when the worst happens – one of the principal figures surrounding the labor and underworld crime issues is murdered.

Carson Reno is very familiar with Humboldt – after all, he grew up and went to high school there. But, Carson has a very successful private investigation business in Memphis and has no desire or reason to get involved. However, circumstances pull him into the turmoil and into a situation that grows more dangerous everyday. By trying to not become involved, he becomes deeply involved and ultimately the prime suspect for the -

*Murder in Humboldt.*

# Cast of Characters

**Carson Reno** - Private Detective

**Rita** - Hostess Starlight Lounge

**Marcie** – Peabody Hotel Operator

**Andy** – Bartender Down Under

**Nickie/Ronnie Woodson** – Owners Chiefs Motel and Restaurant

**Tommy Trubush** – carhop Chiefs

**Jack Logan** – Attorney/ Partner

**Leroy Epsee** – Sheriff Gibson County

**Jeff Cole** – Deputy Gibson County

**Scotty Perry** – Deputy Gibson County

**Elizabeth Teague** – Airline Stewardess and friend of Carson's

**JR Maxwell** – Owner of Maxwell Trucking

**Mary Ellen Maxwell** – Wife of JR Maxwell

**Judy Strong** – Vice President of Maxwell Trucking

**Brenda Patterson** – Secretary Maxwell Trucking

**Gerald Wayne** – Owner Wayne Knitting Mill

**Dorothy Wayne** – Wife of Gerald Wayne

**Nuddy** – Bartender Humboldt Country Club

**Steve Carrollton** – Head of Memphis Mafia

**Bubba Knight** – Mafia associate

**Bobby James** – Mafia associate

**Raymond Griggs** – Chief of Police

**Sandra Petty** – Motel Clerk

**Debbie Day** – News Reporter

**General Samson** – Commander Milan Arsenal

**Henry and Diane Clark** – Patrons at HCC

**Carrie Mae Wilson** – Maid

**James Cole** – Union President

**Lester Blankenship** – Mary Ellen's half brother

**Barney Graves** – Judge

**FBI Agents** – Giltner, Fisher, Turner

# Introduction

**M**y office address is officially listed as 149 Union Avenue – L6, which means I occupy office 6, located just off the lobby of The Peabody Hotel – Memphis, Tennessee. I actually would consider my address to be 3rd Avenue – not Union, but the address has its perks.

The location itself is also handy. All my phone calls come through the hotel operator, which is also my answering service. I eat lunch and breakfast in the employee dining room at a great price. I have a beautiful lobby to greet potential clients - and please don't forget the duck show, it happens twice a day. Aside from the perverts who hang out in the lobby restrooms, I can't find a lot of fault with my office arrangements.

Besides, these are the 60's and people are accustomed to the modern ways of doing business. Appearance is everything, or at least a close second to whatever is first. The new real estate buzz is 'location, location, location' – I think I have one of the best.

The hotel directory and telephone yellow pages show L6 occupied by 'The Drake Detective Agency'. That can be confusing, because the name on my office door reads:

### Carson Reno – Private and Confidential Investigations

I am Carson Reno and always have been. There has never been a Drake working from this office, or any other in Memphis, that I am aware of. However, when I opened the agency I just could not find any rhyme or rhythm in 'The Reno Detective

Agency'. Besides, everybody who has watched Perry Mason knows Paul Drake, and who knows, people may think this is a branch office or something! A little free publicity and promotion never hurt any business, just as long as they call or show-up with money.

A large number of my clients consist of damaged spouses looking for dirt and evidence on the unfaithful partner. It is possible that infidelity has made me what I am today – not a rich man, but I can pay my bills. Occasionally, I get some insurance investigation work – searching for someone who has successfully snookered the insurance company for their own goodwill, or some poor schmuck who filed false claims and skipped. But mostly I deal with the underbelly of our society – where you find some very bad people and never make friends with anyone.

When I'm not specifically working on a case, I try to spend as much time as possible in or near the office. Another advantage of the Peabody is having access to restaurants, bars, shops and the downtown activity. So staying close is never a problem.

Afternoons and early evenings will usually find me at 'The Starlight' Lounge – just off Winchester. Not only is it a good place to 'hang-out', it is a great place to look for clients or, in fact, look for those my clients have hired me to find! 'The Starlight' has live entertainment starting at noon daily. Yes, I said noon. Everyday it is loaded with housewives who use the early part of the afternoon and evening to visit 'The Starlight' for some drink and dance before the husband comes home from work. They cook dinner early, put it in the oven and dance on over to 'The Starlight' for an afternoon of wine and martinis at the 'tea dance'. I have a friend who calls the place "Club Menopause" – I think that is an appropriate name.

Of course with the ladies come the men, generally just in search of some companionship, but sometimes in search for much more. Regardless, these are my clients, or potential clients, and I see no harm in getting to know as many of them as possible.

Rita is the head hostess at *'The Starlight'* and works some unbelievable hours. In fact, I don't remember a time when she wasn't the first to greet me – regardless of the time. She was once crowned Miss Memphis and, as I understand, had a brief acting career. This lady hasn't lost a thing with age; she still has those terrific looks and manner that won her so many awards and titles. No question, she is one knockout and a classy lady who knows her stuff and knows her customers. Rita always makes sure I get an opportunity to 'meet and greet' those who are in 'distress' and might need my services. She's so good at it that I should put her on the payroll – assuming I had a payroll! However, I do make sure she gets tipped properly – whenever I get the opportunity.

My other hangout is home, or close to it. Home is a 12th floor, one bedroom apartment at the 750 Adams Complexes on Manassas. A great place to call home - they have a small grocery/deli on the ground floor and a little bar in the basement called the *'Down Under'*. Regardless of your condition, it is always just a short elevator ride home, and sometimes that makes good sense. Every weekend they offer live entertainment to a usually packed house. Being small, space is always limited. But my friend, 'Andy' the bartender, can always seem to find me room. Last week I spent 4 hours listening to a new talent, Ronnie Milsap. Though blind, I think this guy has lots of potential.

Our story begins on a Wednesday.

This beautiful day in May began not much different than most others. I slept late, up at 11 after too many Jack/Cokes with Andy the night before, then a stop by my office to pick up the mail and check for messages. I had none. I had lunch at the Rendezvous and a few eye openers with Rita and my friends at '*The Starlight*', before finally settling back at the '*Down Under*' to read the mail and hear stories from Andy about the night before.

My mail was typical, the usual junk stuff and window envelopes that never contained good news. There was, however, one interesting letter. It was in a plain envelope with a handwritten address and postmarked '*Humboldt, Tennessee*'. Now, this is both unusual and intriguing. I grew up in Humboldt, in fact my parents still live there, but this was not a note from mother. To my knowledge, this was the only mail correspondence I had EVER gotten from Humboldt – mother was not a big letter writer!

The letter was addressed to Mr. Drake at Drake Detective Agency (I get a lot of those), so they obviously did not know me, or of the fact that I even knew where Humboldt was! I should have quickly realized the potential problems, and simply tossed the envelope and its contents into the trash. Unfortunately, I didn't. Being nosy will always get you in trouble - trust me.

The envelope contained a poorly typed letter and single $100 bill. It had been typed on plain white paper using a typewriter that was in serious need of a new ribbon. It read as follows:


Mr. Drake:

   I have chosen you from the Memphis telephone directory because you offer quiet and discrete investigation in your ad. I am in need of this.

   My husband is being unfaithful, and I require proof before seeking a divorce. Can you help me with this?

   Please accept the $100 as a down payment, and we can arrange a time to meet and discuss my situation.

   My phone number is 784-9847. Please call me if you can help.

   Mary Ellen Maxwell

Not being TOTALLY stupid, I did know who Mary Ellen Maxwell was. She was the wife of, JR (Joe Richard) Maxwell, who owns Maxwell Trucking and Warehousing. The business was headquartered in Humboldt, Tennessee.

Mary Ellen and JR Maxwell lived at 221 Warmath Circle, and to my limited knowledge, they were a significant figure within the Humboldt elite. They have two sons, Lewis and Chuck. This was all public information, and was really the extent of my knowledge about the Maxwell family.

I put the letter in my pocket and ordered another Jack/Coke from Andy. I would read it again tomorrow and decide then if I wanted to call Mary Ellen Maxwell. The hundred was used to cover part of my growing bar tab, and I learned from Andy that my friend, TG Sheppard, would be entertaining next weekend. I looked forward to renewing old friendships at the *'Down Under'* bar.

Andy and I talked baseball the rest of the evening and I took the elevator home sometime before midnight.

# DAY ONE

# Thursday

I woke mid morning with the thoughts of Mary Ellen's letter still on my mind. Standing on my 12th floor patio, I could tell it was going to be a nice, late spring day and maybe a drive to Humboldt and a visit with Mother and Dad would make sense. Besides, I had the hundred from Mary Ellen Maxwell and I had decided to return her money and tell her – NO SALE!

Overnight had brought me to my senses; I knew that whatever Mary Ellen wanted, was NOT something that I could or should be involved with.

~

It was almost 11:00 when I walked into the lobby of the Peabody. When I entered the lobby, Mason Brown was cleaning around the duck fountain, and I stopped to chat.

Mason 'Booker-T' Brown is the headman around the Peabody, and nobody questions that. The labor union just describes him as 'Head Porter' – but Mason takes care of everything. In addition to being totally responsible for the ducks, he makes and coordinates all work schedules for the doormen, elevator operators, porters and parking garage workers. If you aren't a maid or a cook, you best look to Mason for instructions – he is the man.

As always, Mason was wearing his 'Peabody' uniform of gray coat, gray slacks with red leg stripes, white shirt, black tie and a polished gold nametag – reading MASON BROWN– PEABODY HOTEL

"Mason?" I asked watching them paddle around in the lobby fountain. "How are the ducks?"

I normally pay little attention to this well-known attraction in the Peabody Hotel lobby, but this morning Mason seemed a little more determined with his cleaning activities.

"Mr. Carson, I think one day I might just send them down to the kitchen and let that cook put them on the menu!" he said shaking his head.

"What's the problem?" I asked.

"One of them ole' Hens has got diarrhea and she's been leaving her mess all over my clean lobby! I swear I'm gonna' kill that duck if she don't stop doing her 'business' where she shouldn't," he said as he continued mopping around the fountain.

"Why don't you just send her back up to the roof?" I thought that would be a plan.

"Can't," he said not looking up from his duties.

"Can't? Why not?"

"Cause she's my lead duck and wherever she goes they all go. And if she don't quit messing up my lobby, where they gonna' go is down to the kitchen!" Mason said with a chuckle.

~

I was still laughing at Mason when I stopped by Marcie's desk. She was on the phone, so I quickly scribbled a note telling her I would be in Humboldt for the next day or two.

With the phone still at her ear, she read my note, nodded her understanding, smiled and silently mouthed, "Call me later." I would forget to do that.

Then I got back in the Ford, rolled down the windows, tuned the radio to my favorite jazz station and pointed it east on highway 70/79.

I still drive a 56 Ford, left over from college. It's black, 4 doors, V8, manual transmission and nothing fancy. It is, however, very functional and very dependable – not to mention it is built like a tank. It is also very fast. Fast enough to get you into trouble quickly and, hopefully, fast enough to get you out of trouble just as quick.

During the two hour drive to Humboldt, I was trying to find reason with why this lady would have chosen me, or chosen anybody, for that matter. Why not just resolve your own issues on your own terms, and leave everyone else out of the situation? Small towns were a bad place for scandal. Problems almost always appeared larger than they were, and I would advise Mary Ellen to seek help elsewhere – if she really needed it. Unfortunately, I reached no conclusion as to why she thought she needed a private detective. Guess I would need to ask her that question.

~

It was early afternoon when I finally rolled down Main Street in Humboldt.

This normally quiet, sleepy, West Tennessee town seemed unusually busy. More cars were moving along the streets and people hustling along the sidewalks. To me the town appeared to be more crowded than I remembered – I was right.

I stopped by Pullums Bar-B-Q and picked up a pound of meat with trimmings before heading to my parent's house. With perhaps the exception of *'Bozo's'* restaurant in Mason, Tennessee, I believed *'Pullums'* prepared the best barbeque anywhere east of the Mississippi river. However, most of the people that went to *'Bozos'* ate in their dining room – *'Pullums'* was strictly 'take-out'. I figured Dad had already had lunch, but I hadn't and this would give me a good opportunity to have lunch while visiting with my parents.

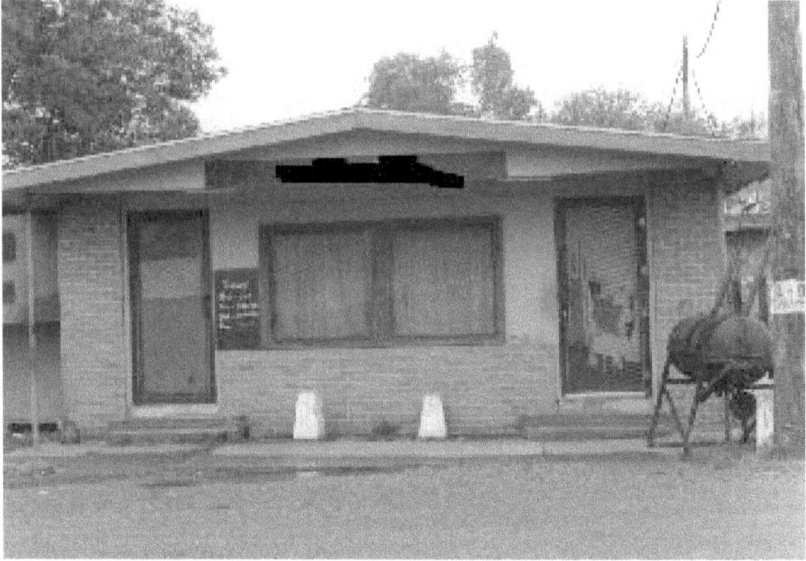

Pullums Bar-B-Q


As I suspected, Dad had already eaten, but we shared a beer; and over the next three hours he and mother caught me up on everything that was happening in this small town.  The local Hosiery Mill (Wayne Knitting) was on strike, which included picket lines, bottle throwing, food tents and a general rowdy crowd around Humboldt.  Evidently, the other local industry, Brown Shoe, was also on the brink of a strike; so, the whole population of this little community was on edge.  It didn't help that news crews, camera crews and the media had latched on to the issues.  Constant news stories and 'updates' flooded the television broadcasts, and both local and state newspapers were using Humboldt's problems as daily headlines.  This town was in a state of confusion.

I also learned that Grannies' (my grandmother's) cat had 'found' another litter of kittens.  Now, mother knows that I know you don't just 'find' a litter of kittens. But, there are just some things she is not comfortable talking about – I understood.  I left the remaining barbeque with Dad finally said goodbye at about five o'clock. They made me promise to stop and see them before heading back to Memphis – I wouldn't keep that promise.

Leaving my parent's house, I drove to 22nd Avenue and stopped at Chiefs Motel and Restaurant to see if I could get a room. Chiefs is a popular local hangout located on one of the main roads that travels through Humboldt. It is actually on U.S. Highway 45, which runs north and south through this part of Tennessee. The busy road is lined with restaurants, motels, shops and businesses as it transitions from a city street to a major highway. Traffic is always heavy, regardless of the hour.

Chiefs is owned and operated by a couple of very close friends, Ronnie and Nickie Woodson. Given the opportunity, you would find it an unusual and terrific place to stay and visit. They offer an indoor restaurant/bar, outside curb service and small cottage rooms for traveling guests. You can't miss it – it's located right under the big neon Indian Chief sign!

**Chiefs Restaurant and Bar**

## Chiefs Cottages

Chiefs was crowded and I almost had to fight my way through the front door. The restaurant and bar were loaded and I really didn't see anyone I recognized, except Nickie, who was working the counter. I waved and she motioned me over, where I managed to find a vacant stool at the end of the bar.

Over the noise and the jukebox I yelled, "Hey, sweetheart, can I get a room?"

"As usual, Mr. Carson Reno, you are a lucky man," she shouted back. "I just had a cancellation, and I'll put you up in Cottage 4. Will that be alright?"

"That will be super, and can a man get a drink in this dive?" I asked looking around at the wild crowd.

"Probably not," she laughed. "I think they have already drunk everything we have. But, let me see what I can do. Jack and Coke – right?"

"Right, and who are all these people?" I asked before she walked away.

"Union people and labor workers, mostly from out of town and here because of the Wayne Knitting Hosiery Mill strike. You hadn't heard about that?" Nickie frowned.

"Mother and Dad briefed me, but I had no idea it was this crazy," I exclaimed.

Nickie shrugged and headed off to make my drink and I continued to observe the crowd. Inside Chiefs bar and restaurant was a place where you simply could not hear anything. In addition to the loud and sometimes shouting conversations, the jukebox never stopped screaming out one country song after another. The noise tonight was not unusual – the overstuffed crowd was.

Ronnie had a small black and white TV over the bar, mostly for sports stuff; however, never any volume. It wouldn't have gotten loud enough to hear anyway! Waiting on Nickie to fix my drink, I watched the muted TV news broadcast from Channel 5 in Memphis. I'm not a good lip reader, but I guessed they were reporting from Humboldt, and about the labor stoppage at Wayne Knitting. The reporter left the screen, and they cut to a live interview by reporter Debby Day. She appeared to be standing on the road somewhere just outside the factory.

Debby was speaking with Gerald Wayne, the CEO and President of Wayne Knitting Enterprise, which operated Wayne Knitting Hosiery Mill in Humboldt. Standing next to Wayne was his wife, Dorothy Wayne, (the former Dorothy Brasfield). Dorothy was an Arkansas native, who had moved to Humboldt with her parents during her sophomore or freshman year - I don't remember which. But, soon after graduation, she moved out of town - somewhere. When she returned a few years later, she brought Gerald with her. I don't think anyone ever knew where Gerald's wealth came from, but he had plenty of it. He and his father, Rufus Wayne, (now deceased) purchased the Hosiery Mill, and it became a part of Wayne Knitting and the Wayne Knitting enterprise. Gerald and Dorothy lived in the old Jones homestead, and have become fixtures in the Humboldt community.

I had met Gerald on a couple of occasions, but only socially. In my opinion he was 'hen-pecked'; however, he seemed like a straight shooter and had a good head for business. I liked him.

Dorothy, on the other hand, was quite different. While it seemed she always wanted to be 'in charge', she had absolutely no head for business. But, that didn't keep her from sticking her nose into other peoples business, and also in other places it didn't belong. It also didn't keep her from sticking 'other things' where they didn't belong either. I think everybody who was anybody had been linked to Dorothy, at one time or another. When I knew Dorothy in school she was a very attractive girl. At 5 foot 9, she was taller than most boys, but knew how to use her looks to her advantage. Watching her on the little television, she looked a lot different now. It wasn't the age, so it had to be the mileage. Dorothy had been burning her candles too bright for too long.

"Here's your drink and the key to Cottage 4," Nickie said when she finally returned.

"What did you do?" I asked frowning. "Did you have to distill this whiskey?" I was not being nice and I knew better.

"Hey, handsome, we're busy. Or haven't you noticed?" Nickie snapped.

Yes, I had noticed, and it was time for me to get out of this bar.

~

'*Night Time is the Right Time*' at Chiefs and it just kept getting busier, and especially busy for a Thursday. Cars constantly circle the building until they can find a place to park, which could take hours. I suspected a lot of the activity was coming from the striking Hosiery Mill workers. It was pretty wild.

After checking into Cottage 4, I walked up to the phone booth outside the front of the restaurant and placed a call to the number Mary Ellen had provided - I got no answer.

I had room service, which I guess is the same as curb service without having to blow your car horn, and called it a day. No wake-up calls.

# DAY TWO

# Friday

**A**fter Ronnie's breakfast of biscuits and gravy, I used the outside pay phone to call Mary Ellen. Again, there was no answer.

Since I really had no client and needed to get back to Memphis, I was getting more than anxious to resolve this issue. I grabbed a coffee to go, and decided to pay Mary Ellen a personal visit. I wanted to return the money and get back to Memphis before the Friday crowd got too big at '*The Starlight*'. While driving to the Maxwell house, I wondered if I REALLY wanted to talk with anyone who might be there.

The Maxwell home driveway dropped sharply from the main road, and came almost immediately to a parking area next to the pool and guesthouse. Only one car was present, a 60 white Edsel, covered in leaves, and didn't appear to have been driven recently.

I strolled up the short walkway to the front door and rang the doorbell of the main residence - no response. The guesthouse was located opposite the pool and I decided to give it a try, too. I knocked at the door of the guesthouse, and again, no response. Other than the ducks on the adjacent lake, there seemed to be no one around.

Walking back to the car and thinking about my next move, I thought I caught movement of someone within the residence - in what could be the kitchen area of the main house. I went back and rang the doorbell again. Again, there was no response – I guess I was imagining things.

Getting a zero here, and really needing to return to Memphis, I figured that seeing JR was my last and only alternative. So, I headed to Maxwell Trucking.

~

Also located on 22<sup>nd</sup> avenue, Maxwell Trucking was a big complex, but with a small modest office. The receptionist, Brenda, was busy hammering on her Royal typewriter when I entered the main office door.

She turned in her office chair, looked up at me and said, "Good morning, may I help you?"

Brenda was a strangely attractive woman that I guessed to be in her early forties and was slightly overweight. Unlike most women, she didn't dress to disguise that weight, and judging by her clothing and mannerisms, she seemed to be proud of it.

"Yes, you can," I answered. "I would like to see Mr. Maxwell. Mr. J.R. Maxwell."

"Mr. Maxwell isn't available. I can make you an appointment, if you wish," she curtly replied.

"Brenda," I responded, "my business is really with Mrs. Maxwell. Can you possibly tell me where or how I could reach her?"

"Are you a friend?" she asked quickly.

I thought I detected an undertone in her question, so I was a little cautious with my response. "Well, yes, sorta. Mrs. Maxwell has asked me to handle a business matter for her, and I need to give her an update. A phone call would be fine, but I can't seem to reach her at the number she left".

"Mrs. Maxwell is out of town," she abruptly replied. "And I'm not authorized to offer any additional information."

"Then perhaps I should speak with Mr. Maxwell, and if possible, it needs to be today. I will be leaving town within the hour," I lied.

Brenda fumbled with a calendar and then looked at me over her dark rim glasses. "Mr. Maxwell can see you tomorrow at 2:00 PM. I'm sorry, but that is the best I can offer. His schedule is completely full." Looking over her shoulder as she spoke, I spotted JR and another lady hurriedly leaving the office by a back exit.

"Okay thanks, Brenda," I said quickly. "Please put me on his calendar, and I'll be back tomorrow. My name is Carson Reno, Carson Reno of Memphis. That's 2:00 tomorrow - right?"

"Correct. Your appointment is confirmed," Brenda said as she went back to her typewriter and I walked swiftly toward the front door.

I watched JR's gray 62 Lincoln leave the parking lot as I exited the front door and hurried down the steps. He was already out of site by the time I reached the Ford and finally got it pointed south on 22nd Avenue. On a guess, I turned right on Mitchell and luckily spotted his car just as he turned off Mitchell and headed north on highway 45, the Trenton highway.

I stayed well behind and followed him cautiously as he drove out Hwy 45 at a very quick speed. Before he reached Fruitland, he slowed and pulled into the Tennessee Motel parking lot. Without hesitation, he put the Lincoln in one of the provided parking spaces and exited the vehicle. I stopped the Ford in front of the motel's small office and watched JR Maxwell.

He walked swiftly to Room 7, entering the room using a key he evidently had in his pocket. He was alone.

Trying to remain inconspicuous, I pulled the Ford back out onto the highway and headed north.

The Tennessee Motel is a single story motel; L shaped with a restaurant on one end and the office on the other. Rooms are contained within the L and Room 7 was almost in the center. It was not well hidden and not very discrete.

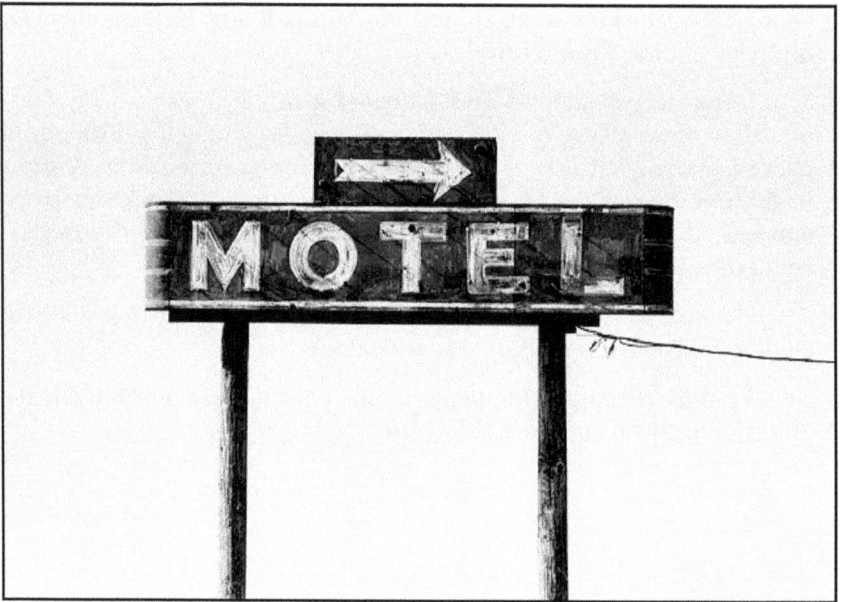

After driving just a couple of miles, I turned around and headed back toward the Tennessee Motel. Across Hwy 45, directly opposite the motel, is a small 9-hole public golf course. They have a large parking area that offers a full view of the motel and its parking lot. That's where I pulled in to observe what I knew was going to happen next. However, what I expected didn't happen.

Trying not to be conspicuous, I was standing next to the Ford while watching and waiting for the next activity. I had a clear view of the motel, but unfortunately, was not able to hide my activities. Thankfully, I didn't need to wait long. Five minutes after JR arrived and entered the motel room; another vehicle pulled up and parked next to his Lincoln. It was a 1955 Chevrolet – ARMY issue! It was painted green army drab with distinctive white letters, telling me it was an official Army vehicle. I watched a tall and stout uniformed gentleman exit the vehicle and enter Room 7 - this is definitely not what I expected!

As I was writing the army car's identification numbers in my notebook, I sensed someone walking up behind me. But before I could turn, I felt something very familiar pressing at the base of my neck – cold, hard and not very friendly.

I am licensed, but do not carry a weapon. My grandfather's .38 police special remains in my glove compartment with a note attached 'DON'T DO THIS'! (OK, I'm just kidding about the note, but I am not armed – usually - and wasn't now.)

"What do you think you are doing?" The voice from behind me asked.

"I'm writing advertising copy for the local paper," I answered raising my hands. "What is the problem?"

"Bullshit, Mr. Reno. Turn around slowly and let's talk," he said quietly. Apparently he didn't believe me!

As I turned, I saw two things. First, that the cold hard impression on my neck was made by a 4 iron, and not a gun; second, that the asshole hassling me was Bubba Knight – a well known, and dangerous member of the Memphis Mafia. Standing behind Bubba, as his backup I guess, was Bobby James. He was another member of that band of crooks. But, I was more concerned and disappointed by the fact that they knew my name, which could not be good news.

Steve Carrollton was the leader of these thieves. He controlled activities from a second floor office on Beale Street, and it is a mystery to a lot of people on how he stayed out of jail. He, and his *Merry Mafia Men*, has their hands in every vice around Memphis, Shelby County and West Memphis. Fortunately, I have personally never had any occasion to cross his path. But now, somehow, they knew me, and what they were doing in Humboldt, is a question I had no answer for - yet.

"Why are you watching General Samson?" Bubba finally asked.

"I'm not. And since you seem to know my name, then you should know who I am and what I do. What is your name, and what do you do?" Bubba didn't seem impressed with my question.

"I've asked you a question, and I asked first. Typically I don't ask them twice," he responded. I believed him.

"Okay, I don't know this General Samson, and have no interest in his activities. I was hired to look into possible inappropriate actions by JR Maxwell, who now seems to be in that motel room with your General Samson. And, that is just what I am doing - looking. You, on the other had, are interfering with my business, and I really don't have to answer your questions – do I!" A strong statement that I was afraid wouldn't stand up – it didn't.

"Mr. Reno, unless you've got golf clubs in this rolling turd you call a car, and want to play a quick 9, I suggest you get back behind the wheel, and go to wherever it is you need to go," Bubba said quietly.

Knowing to whom I was talking, I actually thought that was a good idea. Without other words, I did just as he requested.

Getting back in the Ford, I left the parking lot. As I turned onto the highway, I noticed that both JR and the General had already left the motel.

By the way, for future reference, this 'rolling turd' DID have a set of golf clubs in the trunk. Do you think I should have told him that? I guess not.

I'm just trying to give back $100, and so far not having much success. More frustrating is the fact that Bubba (and I'm sure his other friends) know who I am. Why? Better yet, why didn't I just keep the money and go home? Where is Mary Ellen, and why did she send me the letter? Did she know about my connections to

Humboldt? I had a lot of questions and very few answers. I decided to keep the money and go home, it was healthier that way.

~

Needing some fresh conversation and a drink, I stopped at the Humboldt Country Club before heading back to my room.

It was Friday, and the bar was crowded. Some were waiting to have dinner and some, like me, just drinking. Nuddy had just delivered my third Jack/Coke, and I was standing at the bar talking with Mike Barker, when the worst happened.

JR entered the lower level bar with a lady who simply oozed beauty with every movement. She wasn't tall but compact, with cold dark hair and displaying a manor that suited her good looks. Her black cocktail dress fit in all the right places, and offered just enough to send your imagination into overdrive.

This was the lady I had seen earlier that day at Maxwell Trucking, at least I thought so. Her name was Judy Strong; she had an office adjacent to JR, and the woman I saw leave with him through a rear exit while I waited in the lobby. This lady could stop traffic, but who would want to be driving?

He sat Judy at a table, and then he approached the bar to order drinks. As he walked up and stood next to me I interrupted, "Mr. Maxwell, I need to speak with you. Do you have a minute?"

He looked directly at me and quickly responded, "Mr. Reno, correct? You were in my office today, and I believe you made an appointment with my secretary, Brenda, Mrs. Patterson, right?"

"Right, but it simply won't wait until tomorrow. I have some money that belongs to your wife, Mary Ellen, and I need to return that money. My attempts to contact her have failed, so if you could tell me where to find her, I'll be on my way."

"What? Money?" he stuttered and seemed surprised by my statement. "Look, Mr. Reno, I'll see you tomorrow. As you can see, I am busy," he said turning away from me and signaling Nuddy. His arrogance and comment did not go down well with me.

"If you'll just tell me how to contact Mary Ellen, we can resolve this quickly," I offered with a nod.

"She is in Miami, and I don't know when she is returning. Please see me in my office with a scheduled appointment," he said ignoring me and gathering the drinks Nuddy had prepared.

"Do you have a number in Miami where I can reach her?" I was trying.

"No, and I'm not going to repeat myself. I am busy this evening. Please see me in my office tomorrow. Now get lost!" he said as he turned to leave. This conversation was going the wrong way!

"Look, JR, today has not been a good day. I am just trying to return some money, and I run into trouble wherever I look. Earlier today thugs attacked me, and told me to leave you alone. I don't understand that, but maybe you do. I just want to return some money. Obviously, you have time for General Samson, maybe I should I speak with him?" That was the wrong thing for me to say!

"What are you doing, asshole? You were following me?" JR shouted.

I didn't see it coming. The right cross caught me on my left jaw and put me down across two customer tables and three empty ones; it made a mess. I ended up sitting in the lap of Henry Clark's wife, Diane, while Henry ended up in the floor sitting on his rib-eye steak! Now, sitting in Diane Clark's lap was not the worst place one could imagine being, but with Henry looking up from the floor, it just somehow didn't seem appropriate.

By the time we got ourselves untangled, JR and Judy were gone. I guess I scared him away – huh?

Trying not to draw attention to myself had become a complete failure. I made apology with the crowd, and of course, to Henry and Diane. I paid the drink tabs for the customers whose tables I had unwillingly danced on, and left an extra $20 with Nuddy. On my way out, I stopped by the kitchen and asked Roger to replace Henry's misplaced rib-eye steak. He agreed.

~

It was almost midnight when I finally got back to Chiefs. On the way to my room, I stopped by their take-out bar for a tall boy Colt 45. Not to drink, but to hold that big cold can on my jaw –it helped.

I'd had enough! I was going home tomorrow. I'll just keep the $100, and forget any of this ever happened.

Where does the time go? It's already after midnight, and Chiefs is still rocking with country music and party. Some of these people never go to bed, I guess.

It was hard to hear over all the noise, but I thought I heard a car pull up in front of my cottage and a door open, then close. Based upon the happenings of today, I wasn't comfortable with anything, and I was really ready to get back to Memphis.

I was looking around my room for any kind of weapon when someone knocked on my door. It's almost 1AM and I had not requested any kind of room service!

Of course my gun is still in the car, where it belongs. So, I cautiously opened the door with my left hand while holding my half-full Jack Daniel's bottle in the right. I'll kill them with my whiskey, I guess!

It was Judy Strong.

"Mr. Reno," she said shyly through the partially open door. "May I talk with you?"

"Of course, Miss Strong, please come in." I was in shock!

"Please call me Judy, I will be more comfortable," she said with a timid voice as she walked in my Cottage and I closed the door behind her.

"Okay, then please call me, Carson. So, now that we have our formalities out of the way, what can I do for you, Judy?" I'm still in shock, but listening.

"Were you drinking?" Judy asked staring at me still holding the Jack Daniel's bottle by the neck.

"Uh...yes...I mean no. I mean could I offer you a drink?" I stuttered as we both stood in the middle of the room looking at each other.

"Yes, thank you, but just a small one," she smiled.

"Okay, please sit down and I'll make us a drink while you tell me what I can do for you," I offered pulling one of the small desk chairs from the corner for Judy to use.

Judy started talking almost immediately. "JR, I mean Joe, is in real trouble. I'm not sure why you are in town, and if you are trying to help him, he doesn't think so. Mary Ellen, his wife, doesn't know about his problems, but also doesn't want to help him. I know she loves him, but they just don't communicate."

"Do you and JR – Joe communicate?" I asked handing her the drink I had prepared.

"That's not a nice or fair question," she snapped. "I know what you mean, and the answer is NO! I work for him at Maxwell Trucking as Executive Vice President Sales. Our meeting at the club this afternoon was business, a business meeting. Whatever you said to him set him off like a bomb, I have never seen him act or react that way, ever. He drove me back to my car and never spoke a word, not about your fight or about anything. He was silent, and that is not like JR."

"Well, Judy, what I said to him should not have made him angry. I was just asking to speak with Mary Ellen regarding a business matter, and he went off the deep end," I lied.

"Perhaps he was just on edge," she offered. "But I do know that Mary Ellen is out of town, Miami I think, and isn't scheduled to return until next week."

"You said that JR was in trouble. What kind of trouble?" I asked.

"I'm not sure, but it is real trouble. We've had union officials in our office, from the Hosiery Mill strike, most every day. Then, last week I got a letter from the Army requesting an audit concerning the container shipments we handle for the Milan Arsenal. Then yesterday, I saw some real shady characters leaving his office and they all looked upset, including JR. And Carson, I think they were carrying guns under their jackets. Can you believe that?"

"Yes, Judy. Based upon today's adventures, I can believe some or most of what you are saying." She was getting more upset every minute.

"And this morning, before you came by, Gerald Wayne shows up – unannounced. He marches into JR's office, and they get into an awful shouting match."

"Do you know what they were arguing about?" This was getting interesting.

"No, but I heard Dorothy's name mentioned, more than once. And they were yelling about trucks, the strike, the Army – but I just couldn't put it all together," her voice was shaky as she continued. "I've been there, with Maxwell Trucking, for almost 4 years. The books are terrific and profits are over the top. But, sometimes I wonder where all the money comes from. I handle sales, so I should know the revenue, but when I see the numbers I just question what I read. Something is not right – I just don't know what it is."

"Tell me about, JR. Is he fooling around – involved with another woman?" She knew I meant her, but I didn't say it.

"Carson, to my knowledge he had never seriously looked at another woman, not even me. This is a small town, and if you don't want it known, you best not do it. You know what I mean?"

Yes, I did.

For reasons I will never understand, I told Judy about the letter and about my day. I left out the part about Bubba Knight, but told her pretty much everything else in detail. I explained that I was only trying to return the money to Mary Ellen, and I had no business or interest in becoming involved in anything else.

By the end of my story, we had punched a healthy dent in the Jack Daniel's. She was not only a good-looking woman but also my kind of drinker. I like that in women – good looks and a good drinker!

"Carson, you've gotten me drunk," she said with slight giggle. "Were you trying?"

"Judy, I have simply poured, mixed and handed them to you. The rest you must take responsibility for!"

"I am sorry to have bothered you with my problems," she said as she stood up. "I just wanted you to know that what happened at the club tonight was not JR, at least not the JR I have known for the past 4 years." With that, she walked to the door, opened it and looked at the crowd still around Chiefs. Then she turned around, closed the door and locked it.

It's now 3AM, and the noise outside is still as strong as ever.

"Carson, I don't really want to go home tonight. Can we communicate?"

# DAY THREE

# Saturday

**N**ickie was working the counter when I wandered in the restaurant sometime after eleven o'clock. She, and husband Ronnie, have owned and operated Chiefs for as long as I could remember. He runs the kitchen and does most of the cooking. Nickie handles everything else – including Cottage rentals, the books, and the inventory and keeping Ronnie in line. Ronnie has a 'wandering eye' and probably other 'wandering' parts, which does keep Nickie pretty busy sometimes. However, along with a couple of waitresses and Nickie's supervision, everything always seemed to go like clockwork. She also manages the carhops who served outside patrons.

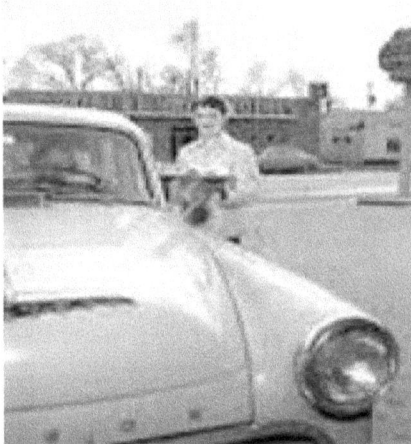

Carhops are a different breed – they are either good or just plain terrible. Tommy is my favorite and has been with Nickie and Ronnie since the beginning. I guess you would call him the 'team leader' carhop. Whatever you need – and I mean 'whatever you need' Tommy Trubush is your man. Everybody knows there is a lot of underage drinking – but Tommy keeps it straight and never lets it get out of hand. I have many times seen him put tough guys on the ground and when he asks someone to leave – they leave.   He runs the outside show – no question about it.

"Rough night?" Nickie asked when I sat down at the counter.

"No, great night but a very difficult day, and I guess breakfast time is over.  Can I just have a burger patty, toast and large milk?" I asked rubbing my eyes.

"Whatever," Nickie said shrugging her shoulders.  "Are you sure you don't need a Jack and Coke?"

"I probably do, but I've got to get back to Memphis, and I don't need any distractions.  However, you can add a fresh bottle of Jack Daniel's to my bill.  The one I have seems to have sprung a leak!"  Wonder why?

"Then you're checking out?" Nickie asked.  "I need to know because we've got a waiting list.  This town is full of strangers, mostly union people I guess, and there just aren't enough rooms to go around."

"Yep, figure my tab and color me gone.  I have no return plans, so it might be a while before you see this handsome face in Humboldt again."  I didn't know how wrong that statement was.

"Speaking of your handsome face, where'd you get that bruise? You been bar fighting again?" she laughed.

"Actually, yes, that is just exactly what I have been doing, and let's not talk about it now. Unfortunately, I got surprised by this one, but it won't happen the next time," I said with some embarrassment.

"Next time?" Nickie was curious.

"Scratch that last comment. I'm outta here today and plan to stay outta here for the foreseeable future. And speaking of the future, what do you know about Mary Ellen Maxwell?"

"Well, well, Mr. Reno," Nickie said peeking over her glasses. "Is that what brought you to town? You have been snuggling up with Mary Ellen when JR isn't looking? Shame on you and you know that really hurts my feelings. You haven't made a pass at me since, well, I can't remember when! Have I really lost my appeal?"

"Nickie, stop that. You are making things up! And besides, what would Ronnie say?" I was trying to dig myself out of this hole.

"He would probably kill you, or at least that is what I hope he would do. On the other hand, he might just say – good riddance! Wanna find out?" she laughed.

"No and please stop this. Seriously, what do you know about Mary Ellen Maxwell?" I asked again.

"Well, she is married to JR Maxwell, who owns Maxwell Trucking and they seem to be quite well off, financially. They certainly have a big nice home, drive big nice cars and take big nice trips."

"Anything else?" I know she knows something, but is talking all around it.

"Like what?"

"Like do they… are they happy in their marriage?" I stuttered.

"Can't say – it's none of my business."

"Please, Nickie, get serious. I've got a problem that I need to get to the bottom of and only information will help. It started simple and got complicated quickly. Anything you tell me is between you and me, promise."

"Carson, it's only bar talk, you need to understand that, but rumor is that JR and this Judy Strong are a number – a big number! If you haven't seen her, she is a 'looker and a taker'. Know what I mean?"

"Yes Nickie, I have seen her and I do know what you mean." Brother, was that an understatement!

"Then, you understand where I am coming from with the 'looker and taker' comparison - right?" Nickie asked.

"Yes, but what about his business?  Have you heard anything?"

"Oddly, yes. These union guys like to drink, and the more they drink the more they talk. It seems that when the Hosiery Mill went on strike, Maxwell Trucking had several trailers backed up at the mill warehouse. The union won't release the trailers because they claim they are full of pantyhose, and their picket line is there to prevent any shipments – coming or going. So there they sit, and as I understand it, these trailers aren't permitted to leave the property."

This was getting stranger by the minute. "Nickie, why wouldn't JR just unload the pantyhose back into the warehouse and remove the empties?  That makes no sense."

"Well, as one union guy said, evidently these trailers are carrying other cargo, and were already partially loaded when they parked at the dock. According to him, they will remain there until the tires rot or this labor dispute is settled. His words not mine. Guess it is leverage they are using against Hosiery Mill management," Nickie said shaking her head and walking away.

I finished my burger patty and toast, just in time to greet Ronnie as he came out from the kitchen. We said a quick hello and good-bye as I threw my stuff in the Ford, getting ready for my trip back to Memphis.

~

Curiosity is a dangerous thing – especially in the hands of an amateur! But I am a professional – right? For that reason, and none other that I could think of, I decided to pay one more visit to Mary Ellen's house before hitting Hwy 79, and my drive home.

The house looked just as before, no cars in the driveway other than the 60 white Edsel; however, something had changed. Although parked in the same spot, this car had been driven since my last visit; the leaves were no longer covering the hood and trunk, and had obviously blown away when someone drove it down the road.

I didn't bother to knock or try the bell; maybe I was afraid someone might really answer. I did take a walk around the pool and into an area at the rear of the main house. That's where I saw what I wasn't looking for. Somebody had recently broken the glass in a door pane and, apparently, gained entrance to the Maxwell residence. Glass was still on the ground and the pane opening was just above the door handle. It was then simple to reach inside and unlock the door.

Making my way back around the pool, I walked over to the guesthouse to see if similar things had happened here. If they had broken into the guesthouse, it wasn't evident. But, I guess they wouldn't need to, because the door was partially open already!

Coming to my senses, and knowing I had absolutely no business here, I walked back to my car and left. I had a two-hour drive to ponder the events of the last two days, and still plenty of time to make happy hour at '*The Starlight*'.

Here's what I know – or think I know.

- Mary Ellen Maxwell has written a letter to a Private Detective asking them to gather evidence on her cheating husband.

- JR Maxwell's closest associate, Judy Strong, gives a very convincing story that Mary Ellen's husband is not cheating.

- JR Maxwell had a secret meeting with General Sandy Samson at an out of the way motel, obviously not wanting others to know.

- However, others DO know because some thugs with the Memphis Mafia were also watching this meeting. Obviously, they knew about it in advance, because they were already at the golf course when I arrived.

- JR Maxwell is very sensitive about his dealings with General Samson. And my jaw is sensitive from his reaction to my knowing about it.

- Maxwell Trucking has some trucks locked in the Hosiery Mill compound and is desperate to get them released.

- Undesirable members of the Memphis Mafia know I am somehow involved, and I have no clue as to how they would know this.

- Judy Strong is a knockout, and I can't wait for a return match!

~

The afternoon 'tea dance' at *'The Starlight'* should be listed as the eighth Wonder of the World, but Saturday night happy hour is something that every red blooded man needs to witness at least once in their life. They say 'it's a jungle out there'. Well, on Saturday night, it is a 'jungle in here'! By comparison, there are at least three 'unattached' women for every man. You will NEVER hear NO when asking for a dance. You will NEVER hear NO when offering to sit and buy them a drink and (I assume) you will NEVER hear NO to any other questions or offers that might be made.

I don't 'fool around' here. Remember that these are my potential clients and that would be bad for business. Besides, Rita watches me pretty close, and lets me know if I start to stray from that narrow path. I do, however, enjoy hanging with old, and sometimes, new friends.

On the flip side, I have an old friend who does 'fool around' here, and especially on Saturday nights. His name is Edgar Woods. He's here while his wife spends every Saturday and Sunday with their daughter in Little Rock. On Saturday night, Edgar is the king of the dance floor; he never misses a song. However, Edgar does one strange thing. When the night gets late and everyone is 'pairing up', he always ends up with someone who just isn't at the top of the 'good looks' food chain, if you know what I mean. I've asked him why and he willingly offers his explanation.

"I don't come here to fall in love; I come here for one reason and one reason only. When they're ugly there is no hassle. They are always excited by the attention, and you don't have to worry about return engagements or getting your heart broken over something that wouldn't work out anyway."

God I love that man!

~

I left 'The Starlight' early and finished my long day at the 'Down Under' catching up with Andy. The Box Tops were playing 'The Last Train to Memphis'. I wonder if they will ever have another hit record.

# DAY FOUR

# Sunday

Sunday is a day of rest. At least that was the way I had planned for it to happen.

I stopped by the office to pick up my mail and messages. Once again, I had more surprises than I really wanted to deal with.

Marcie was handling the switchboard this Sunday and just couldn't wait to share her information. According to the way she was waving at me, I had grown quite popular during my short absence.

Marcie was on the phone, but she managed to hand me my messages and mail as I walked past her and head to my office. The messages were all neatly written on pink message sheets and my short stack of mail included one small package.

Taking a seat behind my desk, I started with the messages. Some new client calls and some old client calls, but not anything that looked promising. I also had a call from Attorney Jack Logan, reminding me of a Monday court date. I work closely with Jack on a number of cases, and also do some investigative work for him. Monday was a preliminary hearing for a mutual client, and much of his evidence had come from my investigative efforts. I had another odd message from Leroy Epsee, Sheriff of Gibson County. Leroy was a friend, but somehow I didn't think this was a social call. However, there WAS a message from Mary Ellen Maxwell!

She had called on Friday (late) for Mr. Drake, and requested a return phone call. The number provided was a Miami number 305-674-8200, room 454. I put that message on the top of my pile and went back to the mail.

Mail was the usual window envelopes, junk mail and a small package with a handwritten address to Carson Reno c/o 'The Peabody Hotel'. It was evidently a shoebox, or about that size, and wrapped in brown paper. No return address and postmarked Memphis, at the downtown post office. Whoever had mailed this to me could just as easily have walked over and delivered the box, saving the $.65 postage.

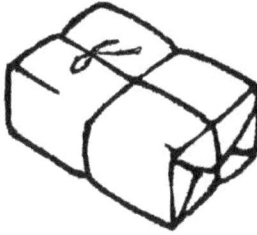

I opened the package, and my initial analysis was correct, it was a shoebox. At an earlier point in its life, it had contained ladies shoes from the Peabody shoe store, just off the lobby on Union. Unfortunately, shoes were not inside the box. I wish it had been shoes.

The box contained a note and cash, a lot of cash. $10,000 cash, in hundred and twenty dollar used currency. The money was wrapped with several rubber bands and had been hastily placed in the container. The note was short, simple and printed on plain white typing paper. It read:

# GET OUT OR GET DEAD

I leaned back in my chair and stared at the note and the money sitting in the middle of my desk. What could possibly happen next? Now I had $10,100 - and still no idea why I deserved any of this good fortune!

I put the cash in my safe, and then focused on the message from Mary Ellen. She had called on Friday, but well before JR and I had our confrontation at the Humboldt County Club. I suspected she knew nothing of any events in Humboldt and was just following up on her letter.

I have a rule to never use my Sunday to return phone calls. In this case, I thought I should make an exception.

I returned her call.

~

An operator at the Beacon Hotel in South Beach Miami answered my call. I asked for and was connected to room 454 – a woman answered.

"Hello," someone replied with a pleasant voice.

"Hello, may I speak with Mrs. Mary Ellen Maxwell please? I am returning her call."

"Just a moment," she responded. "Mary Ellen is on the patio, she will be right with you."

I waited less than a minute. "Hello, this is Mary Ellen Maxwell. How may I help you?" She sounded nice.

"Mrs. Maxwell, this is the Drake Detective Agency in Memphis. I am returning your call and also responding to your letter and the $100 you sent me."

"Mr. Drake, thank you SO much for calling me back," she said with some excitement. "You have read my letter; will you be able to help me?"

"Well, first we need to talk, but not over a long distance phone. We'll need to meet somewhere we can sit down and let me hear your issues, and discuss exactly what it is that you need done. When are you leaving Miami?"

"We are leaving in the morning on a flight and arriving back in Memphis at 2:00 PM." I quickly picked up on the WE in her statement and wondered who the WE might be - a man perhaps? "Would it be possible to meet with you sometime around 3 or 3:30 tomorrow afternoon?" she asked.

Think, Carson, think. "Yes, I suppose we can meet somewhere near the airport, would that be convenient?" I offered.

"That would be great. Where do you suggest?" she asked.

"I suggest we meet at '*The Starlight Lounge*' on Winchester," I answered hastily. "It's close to the airport, and I'm familiar with the place. I should be able to get us a table where we can talk in private."

"But how will I know you?" she questioned.

"Don't worry, I'll know you. Just introduce yourself to the hostess, Rita. She'll take it from there."

"Okay. 3:30 tomorrow then? Let's say 4:00 just to be safe, is that alright?" she offered.

"That will work fine, see you then. I'm looking forward to it. Good-bye," I said putting the receiver back in its cradle

That was a pleasant conversation and I was looking forward to meeting Mrs. Mary Ellen Maxwell. However, I had not changed my mind and would be returning her money. I needed the work, but it would be best if she looked elsewhere or found some other solution to her problem.

Staring at the phone after I hung up, I was wondering if I would get to meet the 'WE' she was traveling with.

~

Still determined to make this a day of rest, I headed back to my apartment. The $10,000 was troubling me, but I figured if someone was dumb enough to put that much money in the mail, then they would be dumb enough to make sure they got what were paying for. I was right.

It is only a short drive to the apartment, but I noticed a 1960 Gray Plymouth following and they seemed to be taking the same route as me. They had exited the Peabody parking garage when I did, and remained behind me 3 – 4 hundred yards back. When I turned into my apartment parking area, they continued north on Manassas. Perhaps it was just my imagination.

I picked up some staple supplies at the deli, and took the elevator up to the 12th floor. After a change of clothes, I was quickly back on a bar stool at the *'Down Under'* talking to Andy. The place was basically empty, and the Bears/ Packers were playing football on the small screen TV Andy had at the end of the bar. He keeps it pretty dark in the bar and I like that, most of the time. Today I would have preferred light – a lot more light!

I had just ordered my second drink when the bar door opened. Momentarily blinded by the light rushing in from outside, I had two bar neighbors before I really saw anyone. Bubba was standing to my left and Bobby standing on my right. I didn't think they came to watch football. They hadn't.

Bubba spoke first. "Carson, how was your trip to Humboldt?"

"Fine," I replied. "As I'm sure you know, my parents live there and I paid them a weekend visit. I was planning on playing golf, but something came up and I missed my tee time." I don't think he found that funny.

Bobby spoke next. "I'm not sure what your involvement is, but it would be in your best interests to avoid visits to Humboldt, at least for the next several weeks."

"Involvement in what?" I still had no idea what this was about.

It was Bubba's turn again. "We have some financial business arrangements in Humboldt that are having some problems. Let's just say they have reached a snag, and we are trying to 'UN-snag' them."

Now that's a new word for me – must be some underground or Mafia language – 'UN-SNAG'. I'm not sure I wanted to know the definition.

Bobby's turn again. "Your snooping around, for whatever reasons, will only get in our way - and most certainly be bad for your health. And speaking of your health, I think our office sent over a payment for your insurance premium. I hope you use it to keep your policy up to date. Health insurance is important during these dangerous times."

"Look guys. I explained to you at the golf course that my business was with JR Maxwell and his wife. It has nothing to do with your business arrangements." For some reason I don't think I made any headway with that approach.

Bubba turned on his stool and was looking me straight in the eye, "Our business arrangement IS Mr. Maxwell. And if you don't stay out of the way, your next news headline will be in the obituary section of The Commercial Appeal. Are we making ourselves clear?"

"Yes, you have made yourself very clear." What could I say? They had!

Bobby's turn, "Look Carson, we have no beef with you. To my knowledge, you have always kept your nose out of our business, and we like it that way. Hopefully, it will only take us a few days to clear up this business matter, and things can get back to normal. Until then, find something else to do, and do it somewhere else – not Humboldt."

With that statement, Bubba tossed a fresh $20 on the bar and said to Andy, "Get this guy whatever he needs, his mouth looks dry." Then he and Bobby walked out the door.

He was right about that – my mouth was very dry.

~

Andy had stood quiet and speechless during my conversation with Bubba and Bobby. Finally he muttered, "Are those guys friends of yours? Sure didn't sound like it, but at least he's buying you drinks – right?"

"Yes, they are great friends, couldn't you tell? They give me money, they buy me drinks and they probably have saved my life!"

Andy went back to talking about whatever it is that Andy talks about. I wasn't listening.

The Packers made short work of the Bears, and I made short work of the evening. After a burger with Andy, I took the elevator upstairs to think through this mess and speculate what tomorrow would bring.

I had an early court hearing with Jack Logan and an early evening meeting with Mary Ellen. I would return the hundred, and explain to her that I was not the right person to handle her issues. That should be that, and I could wash my hands of the whole affair. Good plan.

Oh yeah, I also had to call my friend, Leroy Epsee, the sheriff and see what he wanted.

# DAY FIVE

# Monday

The preliminary hearing went well for our client. I expected the situation to enter one of those appeal cycles where things never seem to get resolved. In summary – it was a good outcome. Sometimes the guilty deserve a break too!

The heat of summer had not yet arrived, so Jack and I paused on the courthouse steps to enjoy the cool fresh air. Jack could sense something was eating at me and nudged my arm as we stood watching the downtown traffic. "Hey buddy, what's on your mind? You just haven't been yourself today. Woman trouble again?"

"Well, yes I guess you could call it that, but not in the way you're thinking. Buy me lunch at the Rendezvous and I'll tell you about it," I suggested.

"Okay, I guess I do owe your lunch. Let's go," Jack said as we started the short walk to the Rendezvous.

Head waiter, Jason, greeted us at the bottom of the stairs and rapidly seated us in our favorite booth. We both ordered the lunch rib special and cold glass of beer.

Jason quickly returned with our beer and I took a healthy sip before looking at Jack. "Listen Jack," I said. "I need you to do me a favor."

"Anything buddy, anything," Jack offered.

"If anything happens to me, I need you to go to my office and open my safe. Marcie has the combination, and I'll make sure she knows that I have asked you to open it. Inside you will find money, a lot of money - cash - all clean cash. Without a hassle, I want you to make sure that money gets to my parents in Humboldt. No questions from anyone, and I don't want that money to get involved in whatever might have happened to me. Understand?"

"Wait a minute. Something happen to you? Cash? Keeping it quiet? What could happen to you? Are you in some kind of trouble?" Jack was concerned.

"Honestly Jack I don't know. Hopefully, most of this will get straightened out this afternoon, and you can forget we ever had this conversation. But just in case, I need to know that I can count on you. Okay? Count on you with no questions, for now. You know me. When this is over, I'll buy you lunch and a pitcher of beer here at the Rendezvous. Is that a deal?"

"Okay, it's a deal. But, please know you can count on me, for anything." Jack was sincere.

"I appreciate that. It helps." I didn't know what else to say.

~

From the Rendezvous I went directly to my Peabody office. I had almost the same conversation with Marcie as I had with Jack. If something happened to me, she was to give him the combination, no questions asked. But, before I finished she started crying and you would have thought that I had just died right there in the lobby!

"Please Marcie – stop crying!" I said patting her on the shoulder. "I just need you to do me a favor that is all."

"But why Carson?" she managed through the tears. "You wouldn't tell me this if something weren't going to happen. You can't do this! It just isn't fair!"

"Marcie, nothing has happened. Okay?    It's just like insurance." (Somehow I didn't like that comparison!) "I just want the best for everyone in case something was to ever happen to me. Understand?"

"Actually NO, but I will do what you want.    But if you don't come back, I'll kill you!" She had managed to calm down some and was wiping the tears and running make-up from her cheeks.

"Back from where, Marcie?   I'm not going anywhere, promise. Just do what I asked, please.   I love you, call you later."

~

Yeah, back from where - that was good question.   I went into the office and called Sheriff Leroy Epsee, as he had requested. This call did not go down well.

As I suspected, his was not a social call.    According to Leroy there had been a break-in and suspected robbery at the Maxwell home and I had been seen on the property – twice.   He wanted to know my involvement.   I explained, simply, that I had paid two visits to the Maxwell home, and both were in an attempt to locate and speak with Mary Ellen Maxell about a business matter.   I also explained that each time I found no one home.   I did NOT say anything about the broken door glass.

"Carson," he went on. "There is more to this.   We know that you attempted to see JR at his office, and when refused, you later had a run in with him at the Country Club.   We also know that you have been asking questions around town about his wife.   You want to tell me what this is all about?"

"Frankly Leroy, no I don't," I answered angrily. "How could you think I would rob the Maxwell residence?   You seem to have a wealth of information without any input from me, so what would you like me to add?"   I was not happy with the way this was going.

"Carson, I don't think you robbed the Maxwell residence, but I do think you know more than you are sharing.   I'm going to say this once, and only once.   I need you to come in and give me a statement.   Chief of Police, Raymond Griggs, is giving me a hard time, and I'm afraid our friendship won't override my duty.   This town is upside down with the strike and labor issues.   Raymond is

68

trying to do his job, and your problems are something he or this town doesn't need at this time. Somehow, JR Maxwell has gotten himself mixed up with the labor unions. We don't know how, but we know it. And now you are accused of breaking into his home. Earlier this week I had Roger Giltner with the FBI in my office, and now they are camped out in town and in our hair every hour of every day. This shit of yours is at the bottom of the toilet, BUT it is in the toilet, and Raymond wants your personal statement. You are going to do this, or I'll have my folks come down and drag you to Humboldt. Are we clear?'

"Yes, Leroy, I hear you loud and clear. Let me take care of a few things here. Is sometime Tuesday okay?" I was confused, but cooperating.

"Tuesday is fine, as long as I know you are coming. I'll let Raymond know. Drive careful and see you then." Leroy abruptly hung up.

'Oh Yeah – See You Then!' Right after Bubba and Bobby get through with me! How could I explain that I had taken $10,000 to NOT come to Humboldt? I'm sure Leroy and Raymond would certainly understand that!

What have I gotten into? Can it get worse?

~

It was 2:30 when I pulled into the parking lot of '*The Starlight*'; Rita greeted me at the door. I told her I needed a private table and a place to conduct business and have an uninterrupted conversation. I also told her that a lady would show up about four o'clock and ask for her, not me. However, she would be planning to meet with a Mr. Drake, not Carson Reno. I told Rita to bring her to my table along with a cold bottle of their best white wine and a couple of glasses. Rita gave me her typical Rita response, "no problem."

Rita found me a table off to the left of the entrance – away from the bar, hostess station and restrooms. It was perfect. With the soft dance music in the background, we should be able to have a quiet comfortable conversation.

I was sipping on my second Jack/Coke when Rita came over to my table at 3:35. "Carson, there is a lady up front who asked for me and said she was meeting Mr. Drake."

"That's right, Rita, that's her. Please bring her over to the table."

"No, that's wrong!" Rita was shaking her head, "Because there are TWO ladies, not one. Do you want me to bring them both over?"

I looked at Rita and thought for a minute. "Yes, I guess so, that's fine. Bring them both over and add another glass."

"Can do," she said as she shuffled off around the corner.

With Rita escorting, the two women slowly approached my table. Traveling from the dim light of the hostess station, to the near darkness at my table - it was difficult for me to see my visitors, but I did my best to scope out my new guests. One lady was quite tall and built like a model, with legs that seemed to go all the way up to her armpits. She was blond, short hair, slim build, extremely attractive, and had her places in all the right places - if you know what I mean.

The other lady was considerably shorter, strikingly attractive and very well put together. She was busty and did a good job of displaying her wares. She knew she was a woman and wanted everyone who looked at her to know it too. She had much darker hair, and like the tall one, had all her places in the right places.

Both were dressed in business attire, medium length tight skits and jackets. It was difficult to see in the light, but I could tell that they were sporting a new tan - obviously fresh from South Beach. And, if it had not been for their expensive French perfume, I bet I could have smelled the tan - it was that fresh. The tall one was wearing a light gray and the shorter one a darker gray. For all anyone knew, they had both just left the corporate boardroom;

however, jewelry just seemed to be hanging everywhere! A 'finger rock' on the shorter one's left hand looked almost as large as a marble. The tall and slim one wasn't wearing a wedding ring, but was sporting a similar diamond on her right pinky finger. Both had diamond earrings, and it was obvious that neither had been shorted on their money tree. These girls had been well kept.

Unfortunately, they just didn't seem to fit in with the regulars at '*The Starlight*'. The good news is this meeting shouldn't take long.

I stood and offered a cordial greeting and a handshake when they reached the table. I guessed the shorter one would be Mary Ellen Maxwell. This was confirmed by her greeting, which was followed by introducing her companion, Elizabeth Teague. Also further confirmed by the initials ET boldly displayed on her suit jacket.

Rita remained at the table waiting on my signal. Beginning small talk, I offered wine, they accepted and Rita poured.

"Thank you Rita," I said signaling we should be left alone. "I'll let you know if we need anything else."

Speaking to my table companions, "I hope you had a pleasant flight. I won't ask about South Beach because I've been there and know it was great, it always is."

Mary Ellen spoke first and looked puzzled. "Yes, we had a great flight and a wonderful visit to Miami. But, I have the odd feeling that I have seen you somewhere before. Have we met?"

"Yes, Mary Ellen, we have. My name is Carson Reno. I'm sure you remember me from high school – Humboldt."

"Oh my!" She seemed more confused. "Where is Mr. Drake? I spoke with him, and we had planned a meeting for here this afternoon."

"Mary Ellen, the person you spoke with was me," I said looking directly at her. "I own Drake Detective Agency. There is no Mr. Drake that I am aware of."

ET spoke, "How odd!"

"Yes, it is odd," I replied. "But that isn't the reason you're here and that isn't the reason I'm here."

"Oh, but it is!" Mary Ellen blurted. "I thought I was hiring a private and discrete detective to look into my personal affairs. Instead, I get some old high school chum, who probably couldn't be private or discrete about anything!"

"Mary Ellen, that is simply not true," I answered frankly. "There is no trickery intended here. You sent me a letter and I am just responding to your request."

"No, I did NOT request you!" Mary Ellen shouted. "I requested someone named Drake, or I would have thought his name was Drake. What idiot would name his business after someone else? I guess you are that idiot – right? Listen, if I had wanted all of Humboldt to know about my business affairs, I would put them in the paper. I would not have some old classmate running around where he doesn't belong and making me look stupid!"

ET spoke again "Look Mary Ellen, let's just go. It's obvious this man is a liar and probably a crook. He's just after money; I can see it in his eyes."

In my eyes?

"Mary Ellen, you could not be more wrong," I pleaded. "I asked for this meeting to return your money."

ET spoke again "Oh sure, and then ask for more, right?"

"Wrong," I replied and then looked across the table at Elizabeth Teague. "And do you mind if I have this conversation with Mary Ellen? Thank you very much."

This comment didn't set well with Miss Teague and she quickly turned up her nose and commented, "Humph."

I turned back to Mary Ellen, retrieved an envelope from my inside jacket pocket and handed it to her. "Mary Ellen, here is an envelope with your $100, and a list of other detectives that can look into your problem. I had no intention of accepting your money. I knew that whatever you needed was not something I should be involved in."

"Oh, so you haven't done anything yet. That's good." Her statement made me draw up!

"Well, not exactly – not much anyway," I said looking down.

"What do you mean 'not exactly and not much'? What does that mean?" She was glaring at me.

"It means I did go to Humboldt to return your money. My parents live there, so it was something I would have done anyway. I wanted to see you personally, or talk with you on the phone, but you weren't there. Eventually someone told me you were in Miami." My words were stumbling all over each other and she was shaking her head as I spoke.

"So, you didn't speak to anyone about this - right?" Mary Ellen asked.

"Well, not exactly." I know I'm in real 'do-do' and getting in it deeper.

"Here you go with the 'not exactly' again. Just 'exactly' who did you talk to and what about?"

"Well...," I was still stuttering. "When I couldn't find you, I went to see your husband. I was thinking maybe he could tell me where to find you."

"Oh shit, Mr. Reno, Mr. Drake, or whatever your name is. How could you be so stupid? Now he knows that I know – I'm ruined!" Mary Ellen was very upset.

"No, no," I argued. "I only told him I was doing some business for you and needed to return some money. He knows nothing about the letter."

"Oh, really! So, just what do you think he thinks when a private investigator shows up trying to return money? He's not stupid!"

"To be honest, I believe he has so many other problems that he isn't really thinking about me right now and probably not about you either." I shouldn't have said that last part.

"That would be nothing new, he never thinks about me anyway, just that whore Judy Strong!" I could see tears building in her eyes.

ET spoke again. "Mary Ellen, I bet Judy Strong is behind all this. Mr. Carson or Reno or Drake – whatever your name is, do you know Miss Judy Strong?"

How do I get myself into things like this? "My name is Carson Reno and, yes, I casually know Miss Strong – we have met." I don't think they believed me. After all, I didn't believe me! Why should they?

ET spoke again. "See - see what I told you? She is behind this whole crazy sham. Come on, let's go, let's get out of this beer joint!"

Mary Ellen took control. "Mr. Reno, we are leaving and I hope I never see you again. I especially hope to never see you in or around Humboldt."

I spoke before they stood up. "Mary Ellen, I need to be honest with you. So before you go, there is one other thing you need to know."

"Okay, let's hear it," Mary Ellen said gruffly.

"You'll hear it when you get back in town anyway, so you might as well hear it from me." These words came out hard. "Your husband and I had a fight - a fight at the Humboldt Country Club."

That's when she put her head down on the table and I heard a muffled cry. Thank God she didn't have a gun! I think she would have shot me and everyone else in '*The Starlight*'.

On the surface, and as they had heard my story, none of this made any sense. But, with Mary Ellen's head down on the table, I had the chance to further talk through what had happened. Eventually, Mary Ellen raised her head, wiped off some tears and seemed to soften up – a little. Meanwhile ET sat quietly with her arms folded, ready to protect her friend, if needed.

I told her most everything that had happened – leaving out my conversation with Leroy, my encounters with Bubba and Bobby and my visit by Judy – of course. Guess I skipped a lot – huh?

But, when I told her that I believed someone had broken into her house, it just became too much. The tears started again and then they got worse.

A trip to the ladies room with ET seemed to be appropriate and Rita sensed the problem and tagged along to help. Thank you Rita.

Tension seemed to have eased when ET returned first back to the table, and I assumed Mary Ellen was still looking for composure in the powder room. She quickly sat down, folder her arms and said nothing. I asked, "So Liz, why is it I don't recognize you – are you from Humboldt?"

"Yes, but I've been away for some time," she answered reluctantly. "I work as a flight attendant with Southern Airways, and spend most of my time in Memphis, Miami or Bermuda. I have an apartment here in Memphis, but do get back to Humboldt on occasion. My parents also still live there, you might know of them. The Teagues– they live on Main."

"Oh yes, sure." I had NO idea who she was talking about!

Finally, Mary Ellen returned with Rita by her side. "Carson, I think she's better now. Please be nicer to our customers," Rita said helping Mary Ellen into her chair and with that silly smile as she went back to her duties.

Mary Ellen had her composure back and looked directly at me. "So, Carson Reno," she asked. "Where do we go from here?"

"We don't go anywhere. You go home and I go back to work. I'm sorry that I have caused you trouble, but my intentions were only to help, please believe that. I promise to never enter your life again." Unfortunately, that was a promise I would not be able to keep

"Okay. Liz and I are going back to Humboldt. As far as anyone is concerned, this meeting never took place. You never got my letter and you never tried to return any money. I'll figure some cover story to tell JR, not sure what, but I'll think of something."

~

Without further conversation, they both got up and left me alone at the table. I sat in silence, watching them leave and then staring at the building Starlight crowd while sipping my wine. They had been gone from the table for over 10 minutes, but their perfume was still there. Amazing.

Finally Rita came over and sat down. "Well, Mr. Detective, it seems the quality of your clients has taken itself up a couple of pegs," she laughed.

"Rita, I wish that were the case. I have done some stupid things in my life, but accepting money from one of them might have been my worst ever."

"The short one I bet." She was observant.

"Yes, but how did you know?"

"Because she was the one controlling the conversation - in fact, she was the one controlling you. Besides, dumb blondes, like the slim one, wouldn't have that kind of effect over you. I've seen you handle too many like her."

"Maybe so, Rita, maybe so," I mumbled. "But if I ever get out of this mess, I'll never get into another one like it. That's a promise I CAN keep."

# DAY SIX

# Tuesday

**H**ow do I get myself into these situations? The bad guys tell you to do one thing and the law tells you to do something else. I guess you can fight the bad guys, but you can never fight the law, right?

Leroy was the sheriff, but he was also my friend. I knew he would never send deputies to pick me up, but he also knew that I would never refuse his request – regardless of the reasons. Besides, I couldn't tell him the 'bad guys' had given me $10,000 to stay away from Humboldt – that would be the wrong thing to do.

I went by my office and told Marcie that I was making a quick trip to Humboldt and expected to return tomorrow. While there, I made a long distance call to Nickie at Chiefs and asked her to hold me a room. Unfortunately, she had nothing available- it seemed the union workers had all of the rooms taken. Of course, I could always stay at my parent's house, but would prefer not to do that. Nickie suggested I try Tyler Towers or the Tennessee Motel.

Tyler Towers was also full, but I was able to get a room at the Tennessee Motel – how ironic. But, at least I had a place to sleep tonight, and I hoped it would be for just one night.

I had really only started my drive up Hwy 70/79, when I again spotted that 1960 Gray Plymouth following – a safe distance behind me. Of course, I knew who it was, and was quite certain they were under instructions to monitor my activities and keep me from going to Humboldt.

It was about 11:30 when I got to Mason, TN. The Gray Plymouth was still following and I decided lunch would be a good idea. So, I pulled into Bozo's Bar-B-Q for a sandwich and cold beer. Besides, I figured Bubba and Bobby were also getting hungry and they needed to eat, too. A happy and well-fed bad guy is better than an angry and hungry bad guy – right?

I took a booth near the back and as close to the men's room as possible.  Bubba and Bobby chose the counter; they were making no attempt at being discrete.  They wanted me to know they were here and would be following me wherever I went.

Halfway through my sandwich and beginning my second beer, I got up, made my way into the men's room and locked the door. The men's room had one of these crazy swing-out windows, and it offered plenty of room for me to stand on the toilet and exit to the back parking area of Bozo's.  Their Gray Plymouth wasn't locked, and I easily and quietly raised the hood.  Then I proceeded to remove every wire I could get my hands on!  This took less than 2 minutes, and I was back in the men's room before B and B ever got suspicious.

Glancing over, as I returned to my booth, I could sense they had gotten a little anxious at my extended absence.  But, fortunately my return brought their tension level back to normal.  They had no idea.

I was taking my time, even ordering another beer after finishing the sandwich. I'm not sure what B and B were thinking, but I wanted them to believe that there was no urgency to my travel. It worked.

Paying my check, I walked directly past them and into the parking area. They were up and only a few steps behind me when I jumped into the Ford and headed West back toward Memphis. I know that must have confused them, but probably not as much as when they hit the ignition on their Plymouth! I'm sure it would take a mechanic several days to put that motor back together. I had a pocket full of plug wires and other gadgets that even I didn't recognize!

Out of their sight and a mile down the road, I turned right on 59 and then north to 54 into Brownsville. There, I jumped back on 79 and headed toward Humboldt. I hope my little trick worked, at least long enough for me to get Leroy out of my hair and get back to Memphis.

Arriving back in Humboldt, I decided to take care of business first. Driving out to Fruitland, I checked into Room 11 at the Tennessee Motel - they were full, and I evidently got a room due to a last minute cancellation. Then, I drove back into town and stopped at the sheriff's office to see Leroy.

Sheriff's Office and Jail

Deputy Scotty Perry was on duty and behind the big desk just inside the front door.

"Hey Scotty, is Leroy available?" I asked walking in the door.

"Hey, Carson," he said looking up from his work. "Long time no see. What brings you to town?" He didn't answer my question.

"Well I'm just not sure, maybe Leroy wants to buy me lunch. We talked yesterday, and he asked me drive up and stop by. Is he here?" I asked again.

"Nope, and I've not been able to raise him on the radio either. Wayne Henley called earlier and said that the cows from the Price farm were loose and running up and down the Gadsden Highway, causing a real problem. If I can't reach him soon I'll have to lock up and go see about it myself. Anyway, I'll keep trying; you want me to give him a message?"

"Yes. Tell him I am in town, and I will be spending the night at the Tennessee Motel, Room 11. He can reach me there or at the VFW. Okay?"

"No problem. What's wrong with Chiefs? All the union thugs got it booked up?" Scotty questioned.

"I guess so. Have you guys been having problems?"

"Yes, and you know it. Fights, busted car lights, you name it and we've seen it during the past few days. Raymond and the city guys are patrolling almost 24x7 out on 22nd Avenue trying to keep peace."

"Leroy mentioned an FBI guy had stopped by. Is that true?"

"You can believe it," Scotty said shaking his head. "Roger Giltner set up camp here a few days ago with several of his agents. I have no idea what that is all about, but they must be staying in Jackson; there are too many of them and no motel rooms around here. I'm surprised you got one."

"Me too," I said over my shoulder as I opened the door.

"Good to see you Carson, stay out of trouble." Scotty added.

He just had to say that, didn't he?

~

The VFW was located on Hwy 45 just outside of town. It was always good for some fun, friendship and maybe some local gossip.

The out-of-towners and union thugs would be in the poolroom or a bar somewhere else – only the locals here.

I found dad sitting with Birdie and the Arnold brothers. We shared a chat and I settled down at the bar for my usual Jack/Coke.

John had been bartender here for as long as I could remember. His J/C wasn't as good as Nuddy's, but the customers were friendlier. Jerome, Roger and Terry were sitting with me at the bar, and from the card room I could hear my friends Jimmy and Larry making noise over some big poker pot.

They had slots in the back, next to the card room, and they were ringing pretty loud. I could see Jane Hopper and Paula Williams sticking coin after coin into the quarter shot machine. In fact, for a Monday, this place was jumping. Many of these folks were workers at the Hosiery Mill, and I guess when they weren't walking the picket line, they were drinking and gambling away their strike benefits – which I know weren't much compared to wages. There is something about a labor dispute that brings out the worst in most everybody. Normally, most of these people would be home having dinner with the family or watching TV with the kids. Now, since they weren't working, it seemed their entire personality has changed.

Bert, Barry and Wayne were having a heated argument over some labor contract issue, and all three had a different point of view. They were getting louder until John threw a bar towel at them and said, "Let's call this one a draw – OK?"

This whole town was still on edge. Things had not changed since last week.

~

It was sometime after 9 when I made my way back to the Tennessee Motel. I found the Ford a spot in front of Room 11 and could not believe what I saw.

Parked in front of Room 7 was the 62 Grey Lincoln belonging to JR Maxwell. There were also eight other cars in the parking lot, none that I recognized.

I had already checked in, but I walked over to the office where Sandra Petty, the desk clerk, was watching a rerun of Gunsmoke on her little black and white TV. I picked up a newspaper and started my conversation with Sandra, "You guys must be booked up tonight?"

"Sure are. I don't know where all these people came from, but we have been full for most of the last two weeks," she giggled. "That really makes the owners happy!"

"I bet it does," I commented. "Say, do you do any long term rentals? I mean like for several weeks?"

"We're not supposed to, but sometimes we do, especially if we know the renter," she answered shyly. "The guy in number 7 must be getting a divorce or something. He's a local businessman and has had the room for a couple of weeks - and just tonight paid for another week. Why? Are you interested in a longer rental?"

"I hope not. Tonight should be my only night in town; I've got to be back in Memphis tomorrow afternoon. But, thanks anyway, and I'll keep that in mind if I ever do," I said walking away.

She had told me just what I needed to know. JR was using this as a meeting place for certain and also maybe a place to get away from Mary Ellen. Speaking of Mary Ellen, I wonder if she had made it home okay. I really didn't want to know. I just wanted to do my thing for Leroy tomorrow, and get out of town before the B&B boys got their car fixed!

My room was just past the corner of the L, and I had perfect site of JR's room from my window. Why do I care? Why don't I leave this alone? Curiosity is a dangerous thing – especially in the hands of an amateur! But I am a professional – right? I think I said that before, and it didn't work out good then either.

I grabbed a coke from the vending machine; some ice from the machine, and then settled down in front of the window with my Jack Daniel's to see what happened next. With the lights out in my room, I had an excellent view of both the parking area and JR's room – Room 7.

Room 7 and JR would have a very busy night.

~

At 9:50 General Samson arrived in his army issue 55 Chevrolet. He got out of the car and went inside without knocking. In just a few short minutes, both he and JR exited the room and walked to his car, continuing their conversation. General Samson got back in his car and left at about 10:00 – almost exactly. He headed north toward Trenton

At 10:20 another 62 Lincoln, this one dark blue, pulled up in front of Room 7. It was Mary Ellen, and she was alone. She also went into Room 7 without knocking, but only stayed about 5 minutes. I could tell she was upset when leaving, because she slammed the door so hard my window rattled. She got back in her car and headed south, back toward Humboldt

At about 10:45 a white Ford Panel van pulled into the lot and parked in front of Room 7. Three men got out of the van and two went inside, again without knocking. The third man seemed to be standing guard or watching the door. This meeting lasted longer than the first two, and they left about 11:15. They took a funny path leaving the parking lot, and I was not able to see which direction they headed on Hwy 45.

At 11:30 a red 58 Corvette Convertible pulled up and parked in front of Room 7. The top was down and it was easy to see who was in the car. It was Mary Ellen and Elizabeth Teague with Elizabeth driving; I assumed this was her car. Both went into his room, again without knocking.

They had been in the room about 15 minutes when I saw a light blue 61 Ford Fairlane pulling into the parking lot. It stopped before parking, then backed up and left, headed back toward Humboldt. Judy Strong was driving!

Just as Judy was leaving, a white 61 Cadillac pulled into the parking lot. The driver seemed to look over toward Room 7 and then turned around and headed left toward Trenton. I did not get a good look, so I don't know who was driving.

Mary Ellen and Liz left the room a little after midnight. They got in the car and Liz was still driving. However, Mary Ellen did not slam the door – this time.

About 12:40 the blue Fairlane returned. This time it circled the lot, and finally pulled up and parked in front of Room 7. Judy got out of the car and knocked on the door. JR opened it, and she entered the room. It was 12:45 exactly.

At 1:00 I saw the red Corvette pull back into the parking lot, however this time it didn't stop. Elizabeth was driving, but Mary Ellen was not in the passenger seat. And for good reason – she was right behind the Corvette driving her Lincoln. She made a pass through of the lot and followed Liz and the Corvette back toward Humboldt.

About a half-hour later both JR and Judy came out of Room 7. They did not speak or touch and walked to their respective cars and left. It was 1:30.

I stayed with it until after 2:00, and nothing else happened and no more visitors to Room 7. Having already had a long day, I went to bed.

# DAY SEVEN

# Wednesday

Something woke me at 4:30. You know, like when you hear a sound while sleeping, but then awaken and don't know what that sound was.

Evidently, the sound had come from the screeching tires of Liz's Corvette. Because when I peeked out the drapes, I just caught a glimpse of it racing out of the parking lot. The top was now up and I had no idea who was driving, or if there was someone in the passenger seat.

Wiping the sleep out of my eyes, I surveyed the parking lot. Most of the cars that were there earlier were still there, and JR's Lincoln had returned to its original parking spot. There was, however, a new addition. The white 61 Cadillac I had seen earlier was back, and was parked in front of Room 3. I assume they had come back and rented a room after I went to bed.

I guess while sleeping I had missed some excitement, and frankly, I just didn't care. Things on this case were out of hand, and I now needed to put things back where they belonged. I needed to get back to Memphis and forget I had every heard of or met JR Maxwell and Mary Ellen Maxwell. Maybe I won't forget Judy Strong, but we could revisit that at a later time! I closed the drapes and went back to bed – I needed my beauty rest.

As you should know by know, I am not an early riser. However, on this day I was up, showered, shaved and dressed by 9:30. This was obviously due to me wanting to get this over with and get back to Memphis. I was thinking, as I stood in the shower, getting up at his hour was not something I wanted to make a habit of.

Throwing my bag into the car I glanced over toward Room 7. JR's car was still parked out front, but the door to the room was not completely closed - it was open about 3 inches. I finished loading my car and watched for some activity from Room 7 – there was none.

Against my better judgement, I decided to walk over and offer an apology to JR. What could it hurt? I was leaving here in a few hours, and it certainly seemed like the proper thing to do - right?

I walked to the room, knocked on the partially open door and called his name, but got no response. When I pushed the door open a little wider, I saw JR.

He was lying at the foot of the Queen Size bed with one foot resting on an over turned room chair, and the other hiding somewhere under the bed. There was a spot of blood on his cheek, and the right eye was missing, as was most of the top of his head. The bullet had entered his right eye at an upward angle taking out three fourths of his brain, along with significant skull and skin tissue. These were all grossly deposited on the opposite wall behind the bed and near the bathroom door. Blood had quickly gathered and then partially dried under where he lay. I would say he had been shot at close range, had been dead 4 to 5 hours and probably died instantly. I never touched a thing.

As I glanced around the room, I saw what I believed to be the murder weapon - a .38 caliber police special, was laying on the floor near JR's left foot. This was a gun just like my grandfathers, which was in the glove compartment of my car – I hoped. Oh shit!

While still trying to analyze the scene, I heard a blood-chilling scream behind me. It was Lucille, the maid, standing at the door and screaming at the top of her lungs - she was frozen in place!

Leaving the room, I practically ran over her, knocking her cart to one side. I needed to quickly see if my gun was in my car. Opening the passenger door and then the glove box - my gun was gone, and I could only imagine the worst!

~

At some point Lucille finally quit screaming and just fainted right where she stood. Within minutes a crowd had gathered, all peeking into Room 7 and the carnage surrounding JR Maxwell. It must have been Sandra who called the police, because they wasted no time in reaching the Tennessee Motel – one city car with Chief Raymond Griggs and one county car – driven by my friend Leroy Epsee. They don't get many homicides in Humboldt, and everyone wanted a piece of the action - and as it turned out, a piece of me.

After knocking over Lucille's cart and finding my gun missing, I knew the worst was ahead of me.  Seeking some comfort, I found myself a resting-place on my car hood and waited for inevitable to happen.  It didn't take long.

Raymond was first, "Okay Mr. Reno, I understand you found the body. Is that correct?" he asked walking quickly up to where I was sitting on my car hood. Leroy was following closely behind.

"Yes, Raymond, I did," I answered reluctantly.

"So, will you share with me what you were doing in his room going through his things?"

"I touched nothing, I know better," I exclaimed. "I went over to his room to talk with him. I found the door opened and then found him just like you see him. I didn't touch anything!"

"Did you touch the weapon?" This was a bad question for me, and my answer was going to make things worse.

"No I did not. But Raymond, I believe that .38 is my gun. Somebody must have taken it from my car, I guess sometime last night."

"Oh boy!" Raymond exclaimed. "One more question before I have Leroy throw you in jail. What were you doing out here spying on JR? We know you had a fight with him, we know you have had contact with his wife, we know you have been to their house and we know you were at their residence either during or immediately after a robbery. Are you stupid or hardheaded, or maybe stupid AND hardheaded."

"That's a lot of questions, or statements Raymond. Where do you want me to start?" I asked timidly.

"You can start by putting your hands behind your back, you are under arrest." Then he turned to Leroy, "Sheriff, please transport this nuisance down to your county jail. This is a county matter, and I really don't want him any where near my office," Raymond said as he walked away.

Leroy was a little kinder, but not much. "Come on, Carson. You know the routine. Get in the car, and you'll get your phone call when we get to the office."

~

At the jail, I made my one phone call to Jack Logan's office in Memphis - of course, he wasn't in. But, his secretary said she would find him and have him call as soon as possible.

I spent the next two hours cooling my heals in Leroy's jail. As jails go it could be worse, I think. He ran a pretty good operation, and I even got some of Pullums Bar-B-Q for lunch, but I couldn't convince Scotty to get me a beer to go with it! Yes, my situation could be worse, I'm not sure how, but it could be worse. I think.

About 1:00 Leroy came back to visit my dungeon. He opened the door, left it open and sat down on the second bunk. "Your lawyer called. He wants you charged or released; I'm inclined to charge you."

"Charge me with what?" I exclaimed.

"Murder," Leroy said frankly. "We have evidence, motive, presence and even the weapon – your weapon that he was murdered with. You even admitted that."

"Now you know that is all circumstantial evidence. I wouldn't kill the guy. Why would I do that?"

"Well other than the fact that you two guys had a bar fight, and the fact that we know you have some connection with his wife – probably rolling in the sack with her while JR wasn't looking. And to ice it, we got a tip you were pulling some blackmail scam on JR. Maybe it all backfired and he ended up dead. We don't have all the pieces but we will." Leroy was talking in circles.

"Blackmail! Where did that come from? Somebody give you an anonymous tip - right? Those go over big in court," I was trying.

"The tipster said JR had paid you $10,000 in cash – hush money. Now, if I go looking for that money, will I find it?"

"Oh shit, Leroy. Listen; do you know Steve Carrollton, the guy who heads the Memphis Mafia?" I was quickly backing up.

94

"Sure, who doesn't?" Leroy answered without emotion.

"Do you know Bubba Knight and Bobby James, two of his strong arm thugs?"

"Yep, know them too. I even had a report there were in town recently. Are you involved with the Mafia too? Carson, even if they don't electrocute you, you will never get out of jail," Leroy was shaking his head.

"Okay, Leroy. I want to make a full confession," I said raising my head.

"That's good, Carson. It will feel better to get the guilt off your chest and save the taxpayers a lot of money. Let me get a stenographer over and then we'll get your story checked out."

"NO! I don't want any damn stenographer," I yelled. "I want to tell you my story, and I won't leave anything out. If you don't believe me, then we'll see the judge. If you do believe me, you'll let me out of here, and I'll help you get to the bottom of this killing and some other things I think are going on around here. Is that a deal?" I hoped.

"No it is not a deal. But I will listen to your story – I am all ears."

"It all started 6 days ago..." And I told Leroy the whole story, start to finish. I didn't leave out anything – not the money, not Judy, not anything. I came clean.

When I finished, Leroy just stared at me. He had that dumb Tennessee redneck look on his face, which I can never read. Until he spoke, I didn't know if I should be planning on the electric chair or getting out of here before dinner.

"You know Carson," he said rubbing his chin. "This helps explain a lot of things, things that we suspected but had no answers for. The FBI agent Giltner has been trying to get Judge Barney Graves, to sign a search warrant for those trucks sitting out at the Hosiery Mill. Up until now, the judge didn't want to get involved because of the union, but this might change that. I am going to get that stenographer, and I want that part of your story in a statement that we can take to Judge Graves. You can leave the rest of it out, because it doesn't concern those FBI assholes. They are on a 'need to know' from both Raymond and myself. However, what you have told me doesn't get me any closer to who wanted, or needed, JR dead and who fulfilled that need."

"Leroy, I realize that, and you know I didn't kill this guy. Don't you?" I asked.

"I would like to believe that you did not," he answered. "Yes, that is correct."

"Okay, let me out. You can call it bail or you can call it whatever. Just let me be the detective I am. We'll get to the bottom of the killing, and maybe turn over some of this other mess in the process. I'll share everything I learn with you, but you need to share things with me too. Is that a deal?" I pleaded.

"No, that isn't a deal either. At least not a deal I would ever admit to. You know that Raymond wants your skin stretched over a log, right? And if he learns that we made any arrangement for an information exchange, I can kiss my reelection possibilities good-by."

"Leroy, you don't work for Raymond, but I know you are obligated to work with him. I'll keep up my end of the deal, promise. And if we solve this thing, you can count yourself a 'shoe-in' at the next election. Besides, just having you believe me is worth its weight in gold."

Then he struck a low blow. "And speaking of gold, what about the money you are holding in your safe that came from this Steve Carrollton and the Memphis Mafia? What happens with it? Are you giving it back?" Leroy was serious.

"Back to who?" I asked trying to change the subject. "We'll cross that bridge later. I just need you, and your deputies, to make sure Bubba and Bobby don't catch me somewhere alone in the dark. I do believe they would kill me without blinking."

"I do too, and I would really like to catch them back on my streets. I'm sure between me, Raymond and Judge Graves, we could find someway to lock them up for a very long time."

Leroy got up and walked out of the cell leaving the door open. He stopped in the hall and turned around. "I'll get the stenographer over and then we'll get your checked out. By the way, how did you like my hotel?" Leroy grinned.

"Food is great, company is fair and the accommodations suck. But, I'll give it a 5 star rating if I can just get out of here!"

"Be patient. It won't be long," Leroy said as he walked away.

At Leroy's request, I gave a four page sworn statement to the stenographer he brought over from the courthouse. Then I made my second and third calls from the deputy's desk phone downstairs. The first was to my parents, offering my assurance that whatever they heard was not true and that I would explain at the first opportunity. My second call was to Nickie. I needed a place to stay and a place to operate from, and Chiefs was my choice.

She promised to hold Cottage 4, and asked that I please get there before she beat Ronnie to death with some unnamed kitchen instrument; he was evidently having one of his better evenings. I told her I was on my way and should see her within the hour. I didn't add that my delays were caused because I was still trying to get checked out of jail!

When I stepped in the front door of Chiefs Nickie just said, "phone" and pointed to the inside payphone. Whatever idiot installed this payphone next to the jukebox had to have been drunk or crazy, probably both. Nobody used this phone because nobody could HEAR while using this phone. The jukebox only stopped playing when Nickie or Ronnie turned it off, which was never. It probably has a thousand county songs already lined up for play. People just keep putting money in it and wondering why their song isn't playing next. It would take a week to cycle through and reach their selection. No matter, they still keep dropping quarters and punching buttons.

Anyway, it was Jack and I have no clue what he was saying. Something about bail, something about Leroy, something about JR Maxwell – I don't know. I told him I would call him back tomorrow and had no idea if he heard me or not.

"Nickie, why don't you do something about that damn jukebox?" I said finding an empty stool at the end of the bar.

"Why, what's wrong with it?" Nickie snapped back.

"What's wrong? It plays all the time and it never stops. 24/7 unless you or Ronnie turn it off. Doesn't that bother you?"

"Nope, like the music. Don't you?"

"Forget it. Get me a Jack/Coke and one of Ronnie's burgers, well done," I offered with frustration.

"Coming up," Nickie said turning to walk away. Then she stopped and turned around. "Hey, that guy on the phone said he was your lawyer. Are you in some kind of trouble, again?" Nickie was being nosey.

"You mean you could actually HEAR what he was saying?" I responded.

"Sure. He first asked for you, and I told him you were on your way. Then he said to tell you that bail had been arranged, and he was filing papers tomorrow to get the murder charges dropped. Then he said you might want to know that Federal Marshals had arrested Steve Carrollton on weapons charges related to something going on at the Arkansas Pine Bluff Arsenal. Then he said your client case got dismissed. Then he said to tell you he was waiting on his lunch at the Rendezvous. Oh, I almost forgot. He also said to tell you that Marcie is still crying – whatever that means. Who's Marcie?"

I just sat and stared at Nickie with my mouth open.

Looking at my expression she asked, "What's wrong? Did I miss something?"

"You mean to tell me that you got ALL THAT from THAT telephone?" I exclaimed.

"Sure. I'm a pretty good secretary, huh? Wanna hire me?"

"Nickie," I said with a smile. "I can only say that your talent never ceases to amaze me. Thanks for the messages, they were important."

"Really," she smiled. "Then who is this Marcie that won't stop crying? Some bow legged woman you left holding a broken heart?"

"No, and it's difficult to explain. She is my secretary, or takes messages for me, and she is concerned that I am in trouble. That's all, nothing else."

"See, I could be your secretary and I wouldn't cry. I wouldn't get the messages wrong either," she laughed.

"Nickie – I believe you. Now, how about that Jack/Coke, I need a drink." I pleaded.

Nickie turned to walk away and then turned around AGAIN. "What was all that stuff about bail, papers and murder charges?" she asked. "Are you in trouble with the law?"

"Maybe, but Leroy and I are trying to work it out. How about that drink," I asked again.

Nickie turned to walk away and then turned around for the third time. "Oh, and one other message," Nickie added.

"You mean you forgot one?" I shook my head.

"No, not from your lawyer. This one was from Judy Strong. She called yesterday, the day before and I think, the day before that," Nickie said rubbing her chin.

"Really. What was the message?" This was interesting.

"Just to call her, that's all she said."

"Did she leave a number?" I had some anticipation in my voice.

"You are kidding, right? I know this woman; she is a 9+ on anybody's meter, and you DON'T have her number? You need to go back to jail – and don't pass GO. You are slipping."

"Did she leave a number?" I asked again.

"In fact, yes she did. When I can find the order book I was using when she called, I'll get it for you; I wrote it on the back. And don't get smart, I really didn't think you would need the number. I wasn't aware you were slipping in your old age!" Nickie laughed.

"Please find me that drink first then find the number. I do need to call her."

"Okay," Nickie said before stopping and turning around for the fourth time. "Hey, handsome, you really didn't kill JR Maxwell, did you?"

"No, Nickie, I did not kill JR Maxwell," I answered with frustration.

"Do you know who did?" she asked.

"Yes. Colonel Mustard did it with a rope in the library. Now get me that number and drink – please!"

I love Nickie, but she can sometime be a real pain. Nickie finally brought me my drink along with number Judy had left and the times she had called. The number Judy left was 784-2724, and according to Nickie, she had last called me at about 1:30 A.M. last night. That would have been about 30 minutes after she left Room 7 at the Tennessee Motel.

~

I called Judy from the pay phone out front.

After several rings a timid voice answered with a simple, "Hello."

"Judy, this is Carson Reno. I am returning your call," I said in a professional tone.

"Are you okay?" she asked shyly.

"Well, I'm out of jail and let's leave it at that. What were you calling about?" I was abnormally cold in my words. I'm not sure why, but I have stopped trusting anybody.

"I need to talk to you. Can I come over?" Judy asked quietly.

"Nope, not a good idea. But what you can do, is tell me what you were doing in JR's room after midnight last night?" I asked.

"Why, you jealous?" I'm not sure where that came from.

"Look, Judy. A man has been murdered and murdered with my gun. I was sleeping less than 100 yards from him when it happened, and the police think I did it. I don't enjoy thinking about the electric chair or spending the rest of my life in jail, so let's cut the crap and answer my question. You will eventually be telling the sheriff anyway. I saw you go into his room after midnight and leave about 1:00AM. For what and why were you there?"

"Okay, but please don't yell or be mad at me. I trust you, and I've shown that." Yes she had, but I just wish I trusted her.

"All right, no yelling and no mad, just tell me about it."

"Yesterday was a bad day at work. JR didn't show up and I was saddled with handling everything. First Mary Ellen's brother shows up…"

"Her brother," I interrupted. "I didn't know she had a brother!"

"Yep, his name is Lester Blankenship, and the guy is a creep and a dimwit. He's from somewhere in Arkansas, and it scares me just to talk with him."

"Judy, wait a minute," I interrupted again. "I thought Mary Ellen was from Humboldt? How could she have a brother from Arkansas?"

"I'm not sure, but I believe she spent her early years in Arkansas – Newport I think – before moving to Humboldt. I guess the dimwit stayed behind. Anyway, I understand he showed up here a couple of months ago and has been living with JR and Mary Ellen. That's all I know."

"Okay, go on," I said quickly.

"Anyway, Lester shows up demanding to see JR. And when he can't do that, he gets loud and nasty. He knocked over Brenda's filing cabinet and kept yelling, 'If I don't get my money from that bastard I'll kill him'. After he left, I called the police. Chief Raymond Griggs showed up and I gave him a statement, and that was that."

"Wait a minute," I interrupted again. "You mean Raymond Griggs knew that this Lester had made threats toward JR, and he knew that yesterday?"

"Yes, that's what I said. Anyway, the day didn't get any better. About an hour later, this bitch Dorothy Wayne shows up wanting to see JR. Again, he isn't here and I don't know where he is. She throws a similar tantrum, but she didn't break anything or make any threats, at least none that I heard."

"Okay, is that it?" I asked.

"No sir, it is not. Only a short time after Dorothy scratches off leaving the parking lot, the union president, James Cole shows up. He's arm in arm with that prick Gerald Wayne. They also want to see JR, and when that didn't work, they demanded the manifests for all Maxwell Trucking trailers that are parked at their dock. Obviously, I did NOT give them the manifests and they left in a huff."

"Humph. Well, did you make anybody happy that visited the office yesterday?" I asked with some confusion.

"I doubt it. Later that afternoon a FBI agent, Roger Giltner, stopped by to see JR. While he was nicer, he was still not happy that he couldn't find JR."

"Where was JR? Do you know?" I finally got around to asking.

"I do now, or I know what he told me. He said he was in Milan, all day."

"Did he say where in Milan?"

"He just said the arsenal that is all he said."

"Okay. Go on," I offered.

"Well, JR has been staying at that silly motel while Mary Ellen was out of town. I don't think he wanted to be around that creep Lester. I drove out there last night to give him my resignation, but when I got there I saw Mary Ellen's friend Liz's car, and figured

Mary Ellen was there too, so I left. I came back a little later, saw JR, gave him my resignation and left. That's it – kaput - nothing else."

"What did he say when you resigned?" I asked.

"That is the craziest part, he said nothing. As I told you the other night, he has just not been himself. It was as though he was listening to me but his mind was a hundred miles away."

"Okay, listen." I said while thinking. "I'm going to have Leroy come see you tomorrow. I want you to tell him exactly what you told me, word for word, don't leave anything out."

"That's fine. Can I see you tonight?" she asked and that hurt.

"No, but you can do me a favor. I need a phone number for Elizabeth Teague. Have you got one?"

"Yes, hang on. But, she is probably with Mary Ellen or Mary Ellen might at her place."

"That's okay, just get me the number."

"Her number is 784-1606. I believe she has a place somewhere off Main Street. Are you going to see her?" I detected some hostility in her voice.

"Just business Judy, just business. I'll call you later. Maybe tomorrow," I said hanging up the phone.

I quickly dialed the number Judy had provided and Liz answered on the second ring with a strong voice. "Hello, this is Liz," she said.

"Elizabeth, this is Carson Reno." I started.

"I know - I recognized your voice. What do you want?" she snapped.

"I would like to buy you breakfast, can you handle that?" I heard her laugh at my question.

"Ha! Most men buy me breakfast AFTER they have bought me dinner. Why the invite?"

"I need to talk with you and it needs to be private. Can we meet?" I asked in a professional tone.

"Okay, where? Wait a minute," she interrupted. "I've got Mary Ellen here with me and she shouldn't be alone. Do you want her to come too?"

"No, just you," I answered quickly. "Find somebody to stay with her if you need to. I'll meet you in Jackson at the Holiday Inn; they have a breakfast buffet. Let's say 9:00 AM. Can you make that work?"

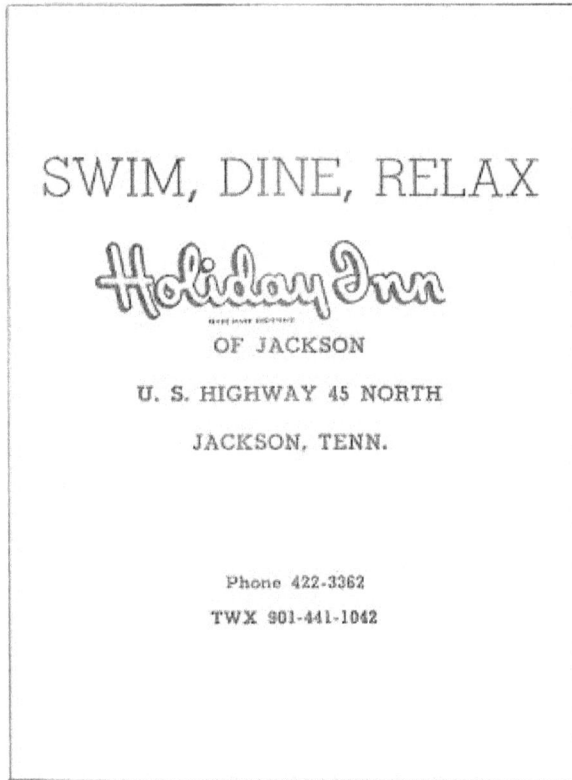

SWIM, DINE, RELAX

*Holiday Inn*

OF JACKSON

U. S. HIGHWAY 45 NORTH

JACKSON, TENN.

Phone 422-3362

TWX 901-441-1042

"I guess so," she answered with a question in her voice. "See you in the morning."

~

Back at the bar, I had another J/C and watched a rerun of the news interview Gerald had given to the press last Thursday. There was just something strange about watching Dorothy standing there beside him. It was even stranger now that I knew that both

Dorothy and Mary Ellen had roots in Arkansas. Was there a connection?

And where did the dimwit Lester fit? How could Raymond have known about his threat and still busted his butt to arrest me?

I had a busy day tomorrow – Day 8.

# DAY EIGHT

# Thursday

It was a beautiful spring morning and I rolled down all the windows on the Ford as I made the half-hour drive to Jackson. This was a 'blue bird' day, with only an occassional white fluffy cloud floating across the clear blue sky.

I had already started my second cup of coffee when the red Corvette convertible wheeled into the parking area. The top was down, and her hair showed the experience of a quick and windy ride on a beautiful morning.

She looked remarkably different from our first meeting, perhaps it was the light or perhaps it was her dress. This morning Liz was without all her frills, fancy suit and jewelry. In the morning light, I could see that Elizabeth Teague was truly a beautiful woman. It was like she had somehow peeled back a layer and was letting more of her good looks be exposed.

Also exposed was that great South Beach tan. She had that golden glow that comes with a new and recent dose of God's sunlight. Medium tan shorts, tennis shoes and a 'not too modest' top provided the viewer with just enough to cause the second look. She was a striking figure getting out of that red Corvette convertible. Where had this girl been all my life?

She slid into the booth like she was sliding under the sheets, then gave me a big smile and said, "Okay, Mr. Reno, what do you want to talk about?"

"Please call me Carson, that will be much easier," I suggested.

"Okay, Carson, what do you want to talk about?"

"Breakfast. Do you want some breakfast?" I was visibly distracted by her presence.

"Just coffee, but you go ahead and eat. I like to watch," she laughed.

"I've had my coffee. Finish yours and take me for a ride in that beautiful car of yours. Can you do that?"

"I sure can, but I don't need the caffeine. Unbutton your shirt and let's hit the highway. You ready?" she asked with a smile.

"Never more ready, let's go."

We had almost made it to the Medina highway before I finally got my seat belt fastened. She liked her speed, and I was enjoying watching her.

"Okay, Liz, here is the deal. I am going to tell you everything I know. Then I am going to ask you some questions and I want honest and straight answers. Then I'm going to ask you to tell me what you know that hasn't already been discussed. After that, you can ask me questions, anything you want. Can we do that?"

"Absolutely, Carson, I am all ears." Which wasn't true. I hadn't even seen her ears – in fact, I had never thought about her ears! But, I'm sure they matched the rest of her, at least the parts I could see!

I started. "I know that you and Mary Ellen visited JR at his room last night. I know that you both came back later in separate cars but didn't stop, I assume because you saw Judy Strong was there. I also saw your car, this car, leaving the Tennessee Motel parking lot in a real hurry sometimes after 4:30 AM, but I don't know who was driving. I know you and Mary Ellen spent most of a week in South Beach, and JR spent that week camped at the Tennessee Motel. I know that a dimwit brother of Mary Ellen, named Lester, has been staying at her house, and I think that may be the reason JR was bunking at the Tennessee Motel. I know that JR was in some serious trouble, but I don't know what that trouble was. I know that Mary Ellen thinks he had been seeing another woman, but I don't think she has any idea who that woman might be. I know that Mary Ellen spent some part of her early life in Newport, Arkansas and I don't think many others know that. Because of this, the presence of her brother has probably been causing her additional stress, over and above the situation with JR. How did I do? Did I get anything wrong?"

"Just one," Liz answered. "She knows who the other woman is!"

"Okay, so she thinks she knows it is Judy Strong, I should have added that."

"I didn't say it was Judy, you did."

"Okay, so she knows who the woman is. And if it ISN'T Judy Strong, then who is it?"

"Dorothy Wayne."

"Please Liz, that doesn't make sense. She's not his type, is she?" I was confused.

"Carson, the truth is Dorothy and JR were a thing before he ever met Mary Ellen. Both Dorothy and Mary Ellen were living in Arkansas and, whatever the circumstances, JR dumped Dorothy for Mary Ellen. Then they ran off to Humboldt with plans to live happily ever after. Then bingo, one day Dorothy shows up with Gerald. Neither Mary Ellen nor Dorothy spoke a lot about Arkansas, so it was never a big item. What was a big item was Dorothy putting the pressure back on JR. I think they probably renewed their relationship once – perhaps more – and Dorothy was using that, and the past against JR."

"Blackmail?" I asked.

"If not monetary, then personal. I think her intent was to ruin him, 'Vengeance of a woman scorned'. Have you ever had that problem?" she laughed.

"Yes, but this isn't about me. It's about a dead man and someone who put a bullet through his eye," I said seriously.

"I understand, and it was your gun that bullet came from, right?" she said taking her eyes momentarily off the road and looking at me.

"Where does Lester fit into this equation?" I changed the subject.

"He's Mary Ellen's half-brother, and I don't know which side sired who. But, when he showed up in Humboldt a few weeks ago, it frightened her to tears. Recently, Dorothy has been using her 'ways' on Lester, and now he thinks he's in love with her and thinks she is in love with him. He is a dimwit and couldn't find his dick with both hands. Sorry, but that is the truth."

"On the day of JR's death, Lester showed up at Maxwell Trucking demanding money. Do you know what that was about?" I asked.

"Only a guess, but I would figure Dorothy put him up to it somehow. Maybe telling him that JR needed to pay him off to hide their former relationship or something like that. Not sure, just a guess."

"What do you know about and what do you think about Gerald Wayne?"

"A wimp, but otherwise he seems to be a nice guy. Most people think he's what you guys might call 'a sex puppet', but I disagree. Dorothy lost those kinds of talents years ago, and I believe Gerald is smart enough to know better. With his money and class, he could probably have most any woman he wanted, so he doesn't need that lush Dorothy for his manhood needs; however, I really think he loves her. With that kind of love and devotion a person can put up with a lot, and he has."

"Tell me about your visits to JR's room on Tuesday night and early Wednesday morning." I asked.

"Mary Ellen had stopped by to talk with him about, I guess most everything. He told her he didn't have time and he would come and talk with her the next day. She left very upset and drove over to my place. We talked for a minute and she convinced me to return with her and try again. I drove her in my car, and we got there sometime before midnight. Mary Ellen told JR that she had asked Lester to move out immediately, and she didn't care where he went, just leave. She also asked JR to come back home, and let her work with him to resolve whatever problems he was having with the business."

"How did JR respond?" I asked.

"He was calm and fairly reasonable. He told Mary Ellen that she evidently really didn't know much about her own half-brother. And that if he didn't leave on his own, he would see that he left otherwise. He told her that his business problems should be resolved before the weekend, and just please give him another few days – then he would come home. He told her he loved her, they kissed and we left. I drove her back home and I went home."

"That's it?"

"No. My phone was ringing when I got home, it was Mary Ellen and she was crying. Lester had confronted her when she got home and was having one of his crazy rages. He told Mary Ellen that JR was going to 'pay' for what he had done to Dorothy and he,

Lester, was just the man who could make it happen. She felt that she needed to warn JR and asked me to meet her back at the Tennessee Motel. That's when we drove out in separate cars and found Judy Strong at his room. We went back to my place, she had another cry and I put her to bed in the spare bedroom."

"So what made you go back to the Tennessee Motel at 4:30? Or was that you?" I asked.

"It was me. I sat and smoldered while listening to Mary Ellen cry herself to sleep. I just thought that if I could talk with and reason with JR, they could save their marriage. When I arrived back at the motel, Judy's car was gone and there were still lights on in JR's room. But as got to his door, I could hear voices, loud voices coming from inside. There was an argument going on and I didn't want to get involved, so I left. Guess my frustrations pushed the accelerator too hard and I unwillingly announced my departure. I went back home and went to bed - that's it."

"Who was JR arguing with?" I asked.

"I don't know and I don't know if it was a man or a woman. I just know it was loud and I did not want be a part of it."

"Okay, so who killed JR?"

"I didn't. Did you?" she laughed.

"Why would I kill him? Okay, so the police have some circumstantial evidence, but I assure you, I didn't do it. And if what you are telling me is true, the argument could have lead to the murder."

"Carson, I don't know. I didn't do it and I know Mary Ellen didn't do it. You're the detective, so detect."

"How do you know Mary Ellen didn't do it?"

"She loved him. She never wanted evidence for a divorce; she wanted evidence to get these leaches off his back. She thought if it were investigated it would come out and soon go away. That is the way she thinks. Besides, she was with me all night."

"All right, your turn. What else do you know?" I asked.

"Look, Carson, when I get ready, I get on an airplane and fly around the world. I can, and do, leave this Humboldt fish bowl whenever I want to. What I know is what I hear from my closest friend, Mary Ellen, and then only when I am in Humboldt. So, what I do know is that Maxwell Trucking was making more money than they had business for. I know that for months the Army was putting pressure on JR to cancel his army transport contracts. I know that some very bad people from Memphis were sucking money from Maxwell Trucking, either commissions or blackmail, but they were getting their share. And when you consider that Maxwell Trucking was still making a lot of money, it adds up to something dishonest, doesn't it?"

"Yes, it does. Thank you for your honesty. Is there anything you would like to ask me?"

"Just a favor, I only eat breakfast from room service. So, the next time you want to have orange juice, coffee and break toast together, please plan accordingly – okay?"

I absolutely had no response! I just nodded.

We had finished our talk and our drive around Madison and Gibson County without a ticket, a crash or running over some innocent pedestrian. For that, I was indeed thankful. She pulled back into the Holiday Inn parking lot and I shook her hand, promising to call whenever I learned anything.

I got out and headed to my car when she yelled at me, "Hey, Carson. Is that black thing your car?"

"Yes," I smiled. "Isn't it beautiful? I have to travel incognito!"

"It works and it is the ugliest thing I have ever seen. I don't and wouldn't want to recognize you! I'll tell Mary Ellen you said hi. She really does like you, even though she might not have shown it. I'll see you later," she said with a wave and a smile.

With that, she sped off on Hwy.75 headed back home, I guess.

Quite an experience and quite a woman.

~

Back in Humboldt, I stopped by the sheriff's office to see Leroy. As usual, he wasn't there, so I left my message with Scotty.

*Please contact and interview Judy Strong and Elizabeth Teague as soon as possible. They have critical detail information concerning the night and morning of the murder. Best you hear it from them rather than me.*

*Also suggest you run a background check on Lester Blankenship. Check Arkansas, that's probably where it would be.*

*Carson*

~

My next visit was to Gerald Wayne. At the Hosiery Mill picket line they told me I could probably find him at home. That is where I headed next.

I rang the doorbell and was immediately greeted by Dorothy; she had a cigarette in one hand and a Vodka Tonic in the other. She appeared to still be wearing pajamas, or some sort of sleeping outfit, and her hair was pointed in every direction but the right one!

"Hi Dorothy," I said offering a big smile. "You may not remember me, but my name is Carson Reno. Is Gerald home?"

"Yes, handsome, I remember you. Went to school together somewhere – I recognize your face. Is that right, didn't we go to school together?" she was slurring her words.

"Yes we did Dorothy. Is Gerald here?"

"Out by the pool. Please go on back, right through the sliding doors. I'll join you in a few minutes." I really didn't want her to join, but it was her house.

Gerald was wearing swimming shorts and talking on the phone. He waved to acknowledge my presence and pointed to a chair, as a suggestion to sit and wait until he finished.

As I took a seat at another table away from where Gerald was talking, a black woman wearing a maid uniform greeted me and asked if I would like a drink. "Yes, a bourbon and coke would be nice – Jack Daniel's if you have it."

When she turned to walk away, I realized I knew this lady. "Hey, Carrie May - Carrie May Wilson, is that you?" I asked loudly.

She turned, stared at me for a moment, then walked over and gave me the biggest and best hug I have had in years. This lady had raised me, from a bottle sucker to Kindergarten. I had not seen her in years.

"Carson Reno, you are a sight for my poor old eyes. How are you?"

"I'm okay, but more important is how are you? Do you ever see Mother or Dad? I know they worship you."

"I haven't seen either of them in a while. But now that I have seen you, I will make a point to look them up. My, my – what a handsome man you have become," she said looking at me and shaking her head. "Do you still pick your nose and wipe it under the couch?"

"Not since the last time you busted my butt for doing that. God, it is good to see you again," I was smiling. "Have you been working here, for the Wayne family, very long?"

"Not really. Mrs. Wayne is difficult and usually her help don't stay around long. Know what I mean?" she said cocking her head.

"Yes I do. I'll put in a good word for you. Go see mother, she would love to see you."

"I will, now let me get you that drink before somebody fusses at me. I'll be right back."

Gerald finally hung up the phone, then walked over and shook my hand. "Nice to see you again, Carson, to what pleasure do I owe this visit?"

"I'm in trouble, Gerald. The police think I killed JR."

"Yes, I heard that. But, how can I help?" he said taking a seat at my table.

Before I could answer, Carrie May showed up with my drink and a refresher for him.

I grabbed Carrie May by the arm and looked at Gerald. "Gerald, I want you to know that this wonderful woman raised me. I'm happy to see her working for you, and please know that I owe her more than I could ever repay. Take care of this treasure; they don't make them like her anymore."

"I hear you. We love Carrie May, don't worry; she is in good hands here. Now, how can I help you with your problems?"

"You can start by telling what trouble JR Maxwell and Maxwell Trucking is in and how it affects Wayne Knitting and Wayne Hosiery Mill?"

"I can't do that. Sorry. First, I really don't know much and second it isn't any of my business."

"That's double talk; you know but can't tell me because it isn't any of your business! That's bullshit."

"Carson, between me and you, JR was into some business that was not good for his health. All of it will eventually be exposed, and a number of important people are going to take a big fall. But you can believe me, I am not one of them."

Just as I said, "I believe you." Dorothy stumbled over to where we were sitting.

"Gerald, aren't you going to introduce me to your handsome friend? We should know each other, but I just can't put a name with his face." She was drunk.

"Dorothy, this is Carson Reno, an old friend. I think you two might have gone to High School together."

"Hello Mr. Reno, glad to meet you. Can I get you some swimming shorts? Let's all take a dip, the water is warm - right Gerald?" She was having trouble standing.

"Yes, Dorothy, but Carson and I are having a business meeting," he said forcefully to her. "You go ahead and swim, we will join you later."

At this point she yelled "Carrie May –Carrie May. My drink needs a refresh and please don't take your usual time. Where are you?" she said stumbling away and headed toward the house.

I was accused of one murder – so what would be the problem with another? I actually could have strangled Dorothy for her words, and done it right there on her own pool deck!

"Okay, Mrs. Wayne, it's on the way. Don't fret," Carrie May yelled from the summer kitchen bar.

Then she added, "Its okay too with you to Carson, right?" She knew I was upset and simply wanted to make the situation go away. Carrie May is one special woman.

"Gerald, is there anything you can add that might help clear me?"

"Not really. JR and I were great friends, and his death will leave a void in our community. Mary Ellen is a terrific woman, and I know she loved him very much. She must be in pieces."

"I'm sure she is, although I haven't spoken with her. It would be somewhat uncomfortable at this point. But, were you aware that she and Dorothy once lived in the same town in Arkansas?" I asked.

"I guess not. Dorothy had already moved from Arkansas when we met, she never mentioned it. How do you know?"

"I'm a detective – remember?" I added.

"Is there some connection between Arkansas, Mary Ellen and Dorothy that is related to JR's death?" Gerald asked frowning.

"At this point, Gerald, I have no idea. Thanks for the information and the drink. Can I possibly slip out the back gate and not go back through the house?" I asked watching Dorothy standing at the kitchen door.

"Sure. Follow the path around the garage and Dorothy will never know you have left."

"Thanks, talk with you later," I said shaking his hand and heading toward the back gate.

I'm not sure Dorothy will remember that I had ever BEEN there; much less know that I had left. As we used to say in college – 'if you are going to drink all day – you need to start early'. Obviously, Dorothy knew all about how to do that. Drunk at noon usually makes for a short afternoon!

I followed the path, as instructed. As I passed the garage I glanced in the window to check out their rides, there were two vehicles. Then I stopped in my tracks!

Nearest the window was a 63 red Ford Thunderbird; this had to be Dorothy's car. On the far side was a 1961 white Cadillac, the same 1961 white Cadillac that I saw parked at the Tennessee Motel the night of the murder!

My next stop was a return to the murder scene. I had a question for the motel clerk, Sandra Petty, assuming she would talk with me.

The parking lot still had a couple of police vehicles; most notable was Leroy's sheriff cruiser. There was yellow crime scene tape across room 7, and that told me their investigation was not concluded.

I would check with Leroy in a minute, but I wanted to talk with Sandra first. She was in the same position where I had found her last Tuesday evening, watching some soap opera on that small black and white TV. I hoped she wouldn't remember me, and she didn't.

"Ms. Petty, I am a part of the murder investigation team, and we have one other question we forgot to ask you earlier."

"Sure," she said looking up from the TV and with a pleasant tone and a smile. "As I told the sheriff earlier, we want to help in any way we can. What is your question?"

"Who occupied Room 3 on Tuesday night?" I asked.

"I have already given the detectives a list with names and addresses of all our guests for that evening."

"I know, but he has the list back at the office, and it would save us some trouble if you would just check one more time. Please?"

"Sir, I don't have to check anything. Room 3 was our only vacant room that evening. We had a late cancellation and did not rent the room for the rest of that night. Haven't I seen you somewhere before? Do you really work for the police? I think you're the guy who was staying in Room 11 and the one who committed the murder! I need to report you to the sheriff!" she shouted.

"Never mind Sandra, I'm headed down to talk with him now. Thank you for your information," I said leaving the office in a hurry and headed toward the Ford.

~

Leroy met me halfway across the parking lot.

"What are you doing here? I know you must know better," Leroy said with angry look.

"I just had a question for the desk clerk. And besides, I can't seem to catch you in your office, so I came to find you. Did you get the message I left with Scotty?"

"Yes, I did. I have a statement from Judy Strong but can't seem to locate Elizabeth Teague. She might have skipped town."

"I doubt it. She and Mary Ellen Maxwell are close friends and she could be at her house. Did you check there?"

"Not yet, I'm saving the widow interview for last. However, we did run an APB and background check on this Lester Blankenship, with some interesting results."

"I thought you might. What did you find?" I asked.

"No open wants or warrants, but there should be," Leroy replied while looking at some notes he had retrieved from his shirt pocket. "He did 5 years in Cummins on a 15 to 20 year sentence for burglary and assault with intent to kill. That means he is on parole, and being on parole, he has no business being out of Arkansas, much less being in Tennessee. I don't have the details of his crime, but we are working on it. I have also sent two deputies to find him and lock him up."

"Leroy, I think he is a dangerous character who can offer some real information about this murder. Were you aware he was a half-brother to the widow and had been staying at their house?"

He looked shocked. "You're kidding!"

"No, I'm not kidding. And did you know that he made verbal threats against JR the day of the murder, and were you aware that Chief of Police Raymond Griggs knew this?"

"Carson you are just full of interesting information today. No, I didn't know about the threats, but I haven't had a chance to talk with Raymond since the murder. Let us get this guy off the streets and then see what he has to say."

"Leroy, I think we will all feel safer with him behind bars. What did you learn from the other motel guests?"

"I've got some statements, but not much. Stop by the office later and we'll discuss," he said walking back toward the crime scene.

"Okay, I'm off checking on some other angles. I'll catch up with you later," I added as I got in the Ford and left.

~

I really didn't want to bother Mary Ellen, but if I were ever going to get to the bottom of the murder, she was going to need to talk - and the sooner the better.

I wanted Elizabeth's help in talking with Mary Ellen, so I stopped at a phone booth and gave her a call, no answer.

It made sense for her to be with Mary Ellen, but where? Surely they wouldn't be at the Maxwell house – well, maybe they might. Maybe Lester had skipped and she had gotten her home back. So I called Mary Ellen's number, no answer.

I figured I would take a ride out to the Maxwell house and see if maybe they were outside or in the guesthouse and couldn't hear the phone. Anyway, what could it hurt? I needed to find Elizabeth and I needed to talk with Mary Ellen.

When I pulled into the sloping driveway things looked just as before. The 60 white Edsel was in its usual spot, and no other cars present. Guess I would need to look elsewhere for Mary Ellen and Liz, but where? I slowly pulled into the Maxwell home parking area and thought about what to do next. Unfortunately, I didn't know the location of Elizabeth's apartment, and I would need to get that information from Judy.

~

The first bullet struck my windshield just under the rearview mirror and then took out my rear driver's side window. Before I ever heard the report, and realized someone was shooting at me, a second bullet struck the windshield again. This one was only inches from the first, and took out my entire back glass. My car had been rolling when the attack began, not fast but moving. I guess this probably saved my life. Whoever was shooting was not kidding, they were aiming at me!

A fast exit was my plan, and when I finally caught reverse, the tires gripped the pavement and I could hear them painting two black marks up the Maxwell driveway. The third bullet struck my right headlight, entering my car through the firewall and finally stopping somewhere under the passenger seat. Somehow I think there was a fourth shot, but it either missed or just traveled through all the empty holes the other bullets had made!

I was in reverse, and I didn't stop when I left the driveway and reached Warmath Circle. I traveled across the small roadway and deposited the Ford in the ditch! Not good! What was good was that I almost struck a Gibson County Sheriff vehicle, as I made my dash across the road.

Habit sent me to the glove compartment to get some defense. Unfortunately, my gun was now in police custody and I had no weapon!

I think deputy Jeff Cole saw his life flash in front of him when my black Ford passed him at a high speed and moving backwards from the Maxwell driveway. When he reached my car, I was already looking for my absent weapon and trying to get out of the car.

"Jeff," I yelled. "There is some bastard shooting at me from the Maxwell house. I don't know exactly where the shots are coming from but I think it is off the right – behind the pool near the guest house."

"Are you hit?" he asked.

"No, just scared," I managed.

Before I could get out of the car, Jeff was already on his radio. What I expected to happen happened quickly. Almost half dozen police cars arrived with full lights and sirens. Within a few minutes, they were organized and entered the driveway with weapons drawn. I waited for that inevitable next shot, but it never came.

What did come was a handcuffed man I assumed to be Lester Blankenship, and he was soaking wet. Jeff and one of the other deputies put him in the back seat of a cruiser. Then Jeff, along with Leroy, walked over to talk with me.

"Before you ask, I don't know," I said. "I just pulled into the driveway and he started shooting. The rest you'll have to figure out on your own. I have three bullet holes in my car, and thanks to Deputy Cole, none in my head. However, I don't know where Mary Ellen Maxwell is, and my fear is that she, or Elizabeth Teague might be harmed and somewhere on the property."

Leroy spoke. "We've checked the house and guest house and found nothing. My guys are still searching over the property, and we might even think about looking in the lake."

"Why is he wet?" I was asking about Lester and I was curious.

"When he saw us coming, the idiot tried to swim the lake and I actually don't think he could swim! Basically, we saved him from drowning. Maybe we should have just let him swim for it!" Leroy laughed.

Jeff called me a wrecker and I asked them to have my wounded car dropped off at Deloch Auto. I didn't think the injuries were serious or terminal, but it was in a real need of some auto-glass work!

I walked over to Leroy's cruiser and sat down. He eventually came over and I asked him to give me a ride to Chiefs; this would give us a few minutes to catch-up.

~

"Carson, I think we have our man," Leroy said as we headed back to the highway. "Convicted felon, parole violation, publicly told others he would kill JR and I expect some blackmail. He is a bad guy. I don't intend for him to leave my jail except for his return trip to Pine Bluff and Cummins prison."

"Did you find his weapon?" I asked.

"Nope, and I assume it must be somewhere at the bottom of the lake. We'll find it, I'm sure."

"Leroy, what did you learn from the occupants in rooms adjacent to Room 7?" I asked.

"Nothing, we can't find them. Both Room 6 and Room 8 checked out early and were gone before you and Lucille found the body. We have the address they left at check-in, but it could take weeks before we ever get to talk to them, assuming the addresses are even real."

"Anything from anybody else that was staying there when JR was murdered?" I questioned.

"An older couple in Room 5 claimed they heard a lot of activity before and just after midnight. The man says he 'might' have heard something like a gunshot sometime during the night, but he wasn't sure, it could have been a dream. Basically, nothing any DA would ever even look at. I've got Lester and a bucket of reasons why he might be our killer and I'm going in that direction."

"Leroy, I don't think he did it," I said staring at Leroy.

"What - are you kidding or crazy? This guy just tried to kill you and we don't even know why. He is guilty, trust me."

"Oh, I'm sure he's guilty of many things, but I don't think killing JR is one of them. Have you been able to talk with Elizabeth Teague yet?" I asked.

"Not yet, but she is on my list."

"There are several things you should know. Elizabeth was at JR's room last night at about 4:30. I said AT – not IN! She heard an argument and decided not to interrupt. Why she was there, I'll leave it up to her to tell you. Also, Gerald Wayne's '61 white Caddy was parked at the motel when I woke and checked the parking lot just after 4:30. Finally, JR and Gerald's wife, Dorothy, was a thing at one time, and I don't mean anything tied to Humboldt rumors. I mean things that happened before they ever knew where Humboldt was. You need to talk with Elizabeth and she will confirm what I am telling you, except for Gerald's car, she didn't see that."

"So Mr. Detective, what are you saying?" Leroy frowned.

"I don't know what I am saying, other than I don't think Lester did it, that's all."

We pulled into Chiefs parking lot; Leroy put the cruiser in park and then turned to talk to me. "Okay, here you are at your home away from home, but I need to ask you to do me a favor."

"Okay, what?" I was listening.

"Stay off the streets and out of the way tomorrow, something huge is going down. It's not solving our murder, but is undoubtedly related. You will just get in the way, and I can fill you in after it is all over. Will you grant me that favor?" Leroy asked.

"Okay, you have your favor. Besides, I don't seem to have any transportation. I'll be walking until Deloch gets me some new window glass."

"Good. That is where you need to be tomorrow. And, by the way, your two buddies Bubba Knight and Bobby James are in town. They got here today, and I expect they are staying in Jackson."

"Oh shit." I said shaking my head.

"Yeah, I thought you would think so. Sleep well, Mr. Reno, we'll talk tomorrow," Leroy said as I got out of the cruiser and headed toward the front door of Chiefs.

~

I walked into a still very crowded Chiefs restaurant and bar. Fighting the patrons, I managed to find a stool at the far end, right next to my favorite jukebox. Nickie saw me and quickly made me a drink without my asking.

I was watching the rowdy crowd when she walked up with my drink and I noticed she didn't leave. She was giving me one of those 'I'm real mad looks'.

"Look, handsome. I know you are an important guy, and I know we dumb hicks here in Humboldt aren't on your level. But if you need an answering service, you get one, I'm not it. I have a business to run, and it seems I have spent most of the day taking phone messages for a Mr. Carson Reno. Understand?"

"Yes, Nickie, and I love you for taking care of my business when I'm not available. You are so sweet to do that. Did I get a call?" I was trying to be as kind as possible.

"A call!" she screamed. "You've been getting calls all day! I can't wait on customers for taking your messages. What did you think I meant?"

"I only meant 'thank you' for taking my messages. Anything important?" I asked with a grimace.

"How the hell would I know," she yelled. "Mostly from your female friends trying to find out where their 'Carson' is. Are you running an escort service from my bar pay phone?" Nickie was pissed.

"Nickie – can I have my messages?" I asked quietly.

"Yes, when I get time. Keep your pants on, or better yet, take them off. It seems you work much better that way! I'll get them and be back in a minute." I actually think Nickie was mad, or maybe just jealous. Either way, she was not happy with Carson Reno.

The 'mute' TV was showing a Channel 5 report on the recent incidents in Humboldt. The union situation, and of course the murder, along with a biography of JR Maxwell, were all being broadcast on television. I got all that from a TV report with no sound!

Fortunately, there was no picture of me and no mention of an apprehended suspect. That was good news, I think. But I'm not sure how up to date these reporters were, things had been happening quickly.

Nickie came back with my messages, all quickly written on her waitress green order pad, just like she was taking a hamburger order.

"First your lawyer, Jack called. He said he knew you were out of jail, and wanted to know if he needed to drive up, or if you needed him to do anything else. He said please call him. Then Judy Strong called. I just started numbering her calls, 5 times today. She just asked for you to please call her. You got two calls from a Liz Teague. On her first call she wanted to know if you enjoyed breakfast and when could you guys do it again? PLEASE Carson – eat where you want, but I know this lady – she isn't your type," she said with disgust.

"Oh really. So you know my type? Anything else?" I asked sipping my drink.

"Yes, a lot else. In between your Judy Strong calls, Liz Teague calls again. This time she left a Jackson phone number, 829-2324, and asked that you please call her. Since that was earlier, I guess you already missed that date. Huh?"

"Please Nickie – anything else?"

"Let's see. Leroy Epsee, the sheriff called, Scotty Perry the sheriff's deputy called and Gerald Wayne, of Wayne Knitting called. Your last call was from a Cheryl Ripe and she left 784-6342 for her return call. And who is Marcie?"

"I told you she takes calls for me at my office in Memphis. Did she have messages for me?"

"I have no idea. She called about 3PM asking for you. I told her you weren't here, and I asked if she wanted to leave any message. She said yes and then started crying again. At some point she hung up and never called back."

"Okay, I'll call her. Did Gerald Wayne leave a number?"

"Nope. I assumed you knew it."

"Nickie, can I have a kiss?" I asked with a big smile.

"No you may not! I've just gotten Ronnie's hands, mind and privates back under control. I certainly don't need to give him any reasons to put them back in motion. It sounds nice, but tonight I'll pass, thank you."

"Nickie – my heart is broken." I said leaning toward her.

"No, it isn't. I'll get you another drink while you see if you can get your harem back under control."

I got some dimes and went to the outside pay phone. I needed to return some calls.

~

My first call was to Judy, who answered on the second ring. I asked her about her conversation with Leroy and briefed her on the day, minus the shoot out, and told her to keep a low profile. I promised to call her tomorrow.

My second call was to the Jackson number that Liz had left. No one answered, but I learned it was the number of the Holiday Inn in Jackson. I left a message at the desk, telling her I would call back first thing in the morning. They promised to see that she got the message.

I had no number for Gerald Wayne, so I would put that off until tomorrow.

My last call was to the number left by Cheryl Ripe. She answered after the third ring. I introduced myself and asked why she had called.

"Mr. Reno – I need to see you about the JR Maxwell murder," she said quickly.

"Oh, really. And just what do you have to offer?" I asked curiously.

"I would prefer to tell you in person. Can you come over?" she asked quietly.

Without explaining my absence of transportation, "Cheryl, I'm afraid I can't do that tonight. But, if you want to stop by here later, I would be happy to talk with you." I was curious.

"I assume your 'here' is Chiefs – right?" she asked.

"Right, I am staying in Cottage 4."

"I'll see you in about 20 minutes, good-bye." She hung up.

It was a strange ending to the call, but I went to my room and made a drink, waiting on Cheryl Ripe to knock on my door. It took less than 15 minutes.

She was a short and cute number, dressed in a very short skirt, tight top and smelled of cheap perfume. I reluctantly opened my cabin door and she quickly entered, looking over her shoulder as I closed the door.

"Cheryl, what can I do for you?" I was cautious but curious.

"Mr. Reno, what do you know about General Samson and his dealings with Maxwell Trucking?" she asked.

"Wait a minute," I asked with a big question on my face. "You came here to tell me something, not ask me questions. I'll listen to you, you talk I listen. That's the way this works. I'll only answer questions after that, if it makes sense."

"Okay. Let me get something from my car to show you. I'll be right back."

Before I could reply, she was up and out the door. Almost immediately the door opened again – it was Bubba and Bobby! How could I have been so stupid! This was not going to have a happy ending.

Bubba spoke fist "Okay super sleuth, we asked you to stay out of town, and evidently we were not convincing. I hope you used that money to pay up your life insurance – your beneficiary will appreciate it!

He took a step toward me and I hit him with a table lamp. Bobby came from the other side, and I managed to cross the bed and avoid his attack. Then they stopped, got quiet and pulled their silenced weapons. Just as I was thinking about all the things in life that I had missed, the door opened – it was Jeff and Leroy! They quickly tackled B and B and the crisis was over. I would live to fight and love another day!

They already had Cheryl in the cruiser, and made room for Bubba and Bobby along side her in the back seat.

"Leroy, you are my hero!" I was ecstatic.

"Carson, you must remember what I made you promise. Stay off the streets tomorrow and stay out of the way. And one more thing, the next time some unknown lady wants to visit your room late at night – give it some thought."

He was right, I would!

# DAY NINE

# Friday

I ordered Ronnie's breakfast special and while it was cooking, used the outside pay phone to call Liz at the Jackson Holiday Inn. She answered quickly.

"Good Morning, again Mr. Reno. Is this becoming a habit, I hope?" she said slyly.

"Listen Liz, if it was your idea to relocate to Jackson, it was a good one, congratulations. However, I need to talk with Mary Ellen today and would appreciate it if you would be available also."

"Okay. What time can you come over?"

"I can't, and for two good reasons. First, my car was damaged yesterday, and I'm not sure when I will get it back. Second, I am under instructions from all Humboldt and Gibson County law enforcement to stay off the streets today. Could you girls possibly make a trip over here sometime today?"

"I guess so; let me check with Mary Ellen. If she is up to it, we'll come over. Should I call you at the number I have been using?"

"Yes, call me back and let me know if she is willing and what would be a good time. Talk with you soon," I said hanging up the phone.

Back at the lunch counter, Nickie brought me a great looking breakfast of ham, eggs and biscuit.

"Nickie, can I make you a proposal today?" I asked as she leaned across the counter.

"Absolutely not. I am just not up to it today, find yourself another woman," she snapped.

"That is not what I meant. I need to camp out here today, and I want to rent that corner booth – for all day. I know it is Friday, and I promise to be finished and out of here before the crowd moves in this evening. How much?" I was reaching for my wallet.

"You're kidding, right?" she said shaking her head. "What's wrong with your room?"

"Several things. For one, I've got some business that just doesn't fit a motel room environment. For another, I need the use of a phone, and finally I need to watch the TV. I think a lot of interesting news will be broadcast today."

"Carson, you are welcome to the booth. Make yourself a reserved sign and be prepared to fight the idiots we get in here that can't read. But, I'm not sure I can put up with you all day. Will I have to serve this harem you have following you around?"

"Maybe, a couple of them. But look at the bright side; I will be here to answer the phone when messages come in – right?"

"There is a silver lining to every dark cloud, that is good news," she said turning to walk away.

"Nickie, there is one other thing."

"I knew it. Okay, shoot. No, no, no, wait. I didn't mean to use the word shoot. What is this other thing?" she laughed.

"Here is a $20 bill, and I have taken the liberty of making this 'Out of Order' sign for the jukebox. I can't handle that noise and conduct business at the same time. Again, I promise to be out of you hair before the crowd gets here this afternoon. Can we do that?"

"You are crazy. Do you know that? You mean to tell me I must spend all day with no music? And let me guess, you are going to want me to turn the volume up on the TV, right? I'll talk to Ronnie and see how much he wants to sell this place. You can just buy it today and do whatever you want." Nickie was being difficult.

"Chiefs would not be Chiefs with you – and you know it. How about it – we got a deal?" I pleaded.

"Okay, handsome. We have a deal until the first fight starts over the phone, the booth, the TV or the jukebox. When that happens, our deal is off and you get out of here – understand?"

"Understood, and you are a sweetheart. And if you ever decide to leave Ronnie, I hope you would give me a chance."

"Carson, you are an idiot. Stop with the flattery, at least stop until I get the jukebox unplugged. Then you can restart where you left off."

~

Now I had a base of operation for the day, and next I needed to find out about transportation. I called Deloch Auto and spoke with Charles, who said that the windshield and back window could be replaced today. If I needed the back door window and the other bullet damage fixed, it would be sometime next week. We agreed to fix the major damage, and put something in the back door window to keep the weather out. The bullet damage we would take care of later, I needed transportation. Charles said it would be ready sometime this afternoon, and he would call me at Chiefs when it was ready.

A call to information got me the home number for Gerald Wayne. For reasons, I can never understand, these pay phones never have a directory with them – just that little black chain hanging there where the phone book used to be attached! They give phone books away, so why would anybody steal one? Phone book bandits needed to be punished! I promised myself to look into it when I had time.

Carrie May answered, and after our hellos, I asked if Gerald was available – he was not. But she promised to give him my number, and have him call as soon as he came in. I could hear Dorothy in the background screaming "Who is it? Is it for me?" It was just after 9 AM, and I wondered if this was a new drunk or still the one left over from last night!

I gave my love to Carrie May and promised to not let us lose touch again. Dorothy was still yelling in the background when she hung up. I may still kill that woman yet; I had not ruled that out.

Back inside at my new office, Nickie had moved my breakfast special over to my new desk.

"Can I warm that for you?" she asked.

"Yes, please - and more coffee. Also, would you mind turning up the TV and put it on Channel 5 news?"

"Yes sir and I promise not to bow, although the thought did occur to me! I guess now that we have moved up in class, Ronnie and I need to talk about raising our menu prices – ya' think?"

134

"Well, sweetheart, class has its benefits," I replied ignoring her silliness. "Now, just turn up the TV. I did say please, didn't I?"

"No, but I didn't notice. You usually don't."

~

The news had nothing about Humboldt, but somehow I expected things were happening that had just not yet caught up with the news. I was right.

Jack Logan called early. When he got over his surprise at me actually being available to talk with him and not having to leave a message, he wanted to know if I was involved in what was going down today. After some detailed explanation, Jack was comfortable that my level of involvement was not serious, but I would probably be a part of the legal process when it began to move forward. He said he would make a few calls, and suggested that I get my ass back to Memphis as quickly as I could. I agreed, but let him know that I intended to walk away from here with the JR murder solved and my name cleared. We made plans to talk later that afternoon, after the fireworks.

Liz called next, and wanted to know if lunchtime would be okay. I said that would be fine and told her about my 'office for the day' and that we should meet here.

"Carson," she screamed. "We don't DO Chiefs. You will need to make other arrangements. Sorry."

"Look, leave your jewelry at home, put on your jeans and see how the real world manages to exist." I wanted to add 'you can leave the rollers in your hair and no one will recognize you or even care', but thought I better quit while I was winning.

"Okay, but I'm keeping my sunglasses on, and I'm not parking where someone might see my car," she quipped.

"Fine, I'll see you for lunch. I think Escargot is the special for the day!"

At that point, I think she hung up on me. Resisting the temptation to ask Nickie if she could whip up some escargot for my guests, I did get her to switch the TV around through the two other channels. They had nothing about Humboldt, so we went back to Channel 5.

Next, Judy called and she was very upset - the FBI was in her office. They were searching all records and ordered her to close the front door and lock it. Any trucks in transit were to immediately return to the Humboldt terminal without stops. They also told her that agents would be stopping all Maxwell Trucking vehicles found traveling the highways, and provide escort back to the Humboldt terminal. Adding to the embarrassment, Agent Giltner searched her office along with her purse and her person (he was being an asshole and this was just meant to intimidate). Brenda's files, purse and person were also searched, and both had been placed in the conference room with instructions to remain there until told differently. Dispatcher, Tom Harbin, had been confined to his dock office and not permitted to leave, use the phone or the radio without a FBI agent present.

She was calling me from the conference room phone and was scared to death of being arrested. I told her to just calm down, she had nothing to fear and to call me back when they released her. I wasn't sure I believed that 'nothing to fear' statement, but she needed to calm down.

It had started.

~

Gerald Wayne's white Cadillac pulled up in front of Chiefs, and he entered by the restaurant door. He spotted me immediately and came over to sit down.

"You wanted to talk?" he was curt. "You better make it quick. I think I am in for a busy day."

"What was your car doing parked at the Tennessee Motel on the night of JR's murder?" I asked without hesitation.

The blood left his face and he got white as a sheet. Nickie had started over to the table, when she saw me wave my hand letting her know that this was not a good time for her to say 'may I help you'.

"What time was it there?" he asked.

"I saw it at 4:30. And that will probably be determined to be somewhere close to the time of death."

"It wasn't me." He was shaking.

"Who was driving your car that night? And don't embarrass me by saying you don't know."

He said it anyway!

"I don't know."

"Look, Gerald, it is going to come out. Was Dorothy driving your car? Could it have been Lester driving your car?"

"I really mean it. I don't know. She was really drunk that day. We had an argument, and for some reason, she took my car. The keys hang by the back door, and I didn't think that was too unusual. But she was out all night. I took her car to my office the next morning, and when I returned home later, the car was back and she was in bed. So I really don't know. Carson, I love Dorothy and she is just not capable – I mean do you suspect her?"

I never got a chance to respond. While he had been talking a Gray Plymouth with government tags pulled up next to his car. Two large guys wearing gray suits, conservative ties and sunglasses got out and headed to the door. They were FBI, and you could have picked them out in any crowd.

They walked over to our table – the black agent spoke. "Mr. Wayne, I'm agent Fisher and this is agent Turner. We have a warrant for your arrest, and you need to come with us. We are taking you to the FBI office in Jackson. There, you will be given the opportunity to make a phone call. Agent Turner will be driving your car, so we will need the keys. We can avoid handcuffs if you cooperate; otherwise we are prepared to bring you in by any means necessary."

Strangely calm, Gerald spoke, "I will cooperate."

He handed them the keys and they left without any other words. Neither of them ever looked at me, it was almost as if I was invisible. For once, I was not disappointed to not be noticed.

Nickie walked over to the table. "Wow, does this stuff go on in your office all the time?"

"Fortunately, no. Hey, go turn up the TV – I think things are going to get interesting."

A TV reporter was broadcasting live from the street across from the Hosiery Mill. She was reporting on the FBI removing Maxwell Trucking trailers from the docking area. The union was visibly protesting, and they were throwing rocks and bottles at the rigs as they were being driven out the gates and down 22nd avenue.

The TV then switched to another remote reporter who seemed to be standing at the gates of a military installation; it was the Milan Arsenal. The camera caught a glimpse of General Samson in the back of another FBI Gray Plymouth; they offered no information about why or where he was being taken. They would report more when additional details became available.

The next cut was to the front of Maxwell Trucking, and I could not help but think of Judy sitting in that building wondering about her future and wondering what would happen next.

The shot and commentary were about the trucks from Wayne Knitting Hosiery Mill being rolled into the terminal and behind the gates. You could see FBI agents in their gray suits and sunglasses standing guard at the gate. They had no information about the contents of these trucks and would report more when additional details became available.

The phone rang again. Nickie answered and it was for me – Sheriff Leroy Epsee was checking up on me. I told him my routine and he seemed pleased. He hung up, saying he would see me later that afternoon.

~

I was walking back to my table when the door opened and in walked Mary Ellen and Elizabeth – I think! They were wearing ill fitting jeans, something that looked like cowboy shirts and had their hair in some silly bun sitting on top of their heads. I really wasn't sure who it was. Maybe it was Annie Oakley and Penny from Sky King, or maybe just some local rednecks in drag! If it was their intent to be discrete and unnoticed they had failed miserably.

From behind the dark sunglasses I heard, "Mr. Carson, we are here as you requested."

I'm trying to avoid hysterical laughter and managed to just show a small giggle. "Ladies, please step into my office." I took them to my corner booth.

"Mary Ellen, thank you for coming, and I know it is a terrible time for you," I said sincerely. "Please accept my sympathy for your loss and my respect for your grief. I promise I would not have asked to see you if I didn't think it to be important."

She managed to speak, "I understand. What can I do for you?"

Liz jumped in. "Yes, and I hope whatever we can do for you doesn't involve eating, because if you think my lips would touch this food – well, then you don't know my lips!"

I had a great comeback regarding her lips, but really needed to keep this meeting headed in another direction.

"I want to solve your husband's murder, and I have a plan to bring the guilty person out into the open. But I will need your cooperation."

"I thought they had the guilty person. Didn't they arrest my half-bother for the murder?" Mary Ellen uttered.

"No, not really," I answered shaking my head. "He has been arrested for a number of offenses, but not charged with your husband's murder. I don't think he did it, but unless we can prove otherwise, he will probably be charged and probably be convicted. If he is guilty, there won't be any harm in my plan. If he isn't guilty, then I hope my plan will expose the one who is. Will you help?"

"Carson, I will do whatever is necessary," Mary Ellen said quietly. "For some strange reason I trust you, probably because Liz has convinced me that I should. So, yes. What do you need?"

Then I explained my plan to both Mary Ellen and Liz. I ended by telling her that Leroy would be calling and visiting with her, probably later today. It would be better if she could move herself back in the Warmath Circle house. She agreed, and said they would be doing that later today.

Still in disguise, they made their way out the door and off to somewhere. I never saw Liz's car. Who knows – they may have taken a cab? Although if I were a cab driver, I probably would not have given them a ride!

Nickie walked over. "My God Carson, who were those two? The Carnival will be here next week for the Festival, are they early arrivals?"

"Hey, Nickie, I thought they were a couple of your regulars? You didn't recognize them?"

She threw a menu at me, but fortunately it missed.

~

I had missed a lot of TV announcements while talking with Mary Ellen and Liz, so I had to wait for them to recycle. I didn't have long to wait.

In summary, the FBI had seized the assets of Maxwell Trucking. These included partially loaded trailers parked at Wayne Knitting Hosiery Mill, The Milan Arsenal and The Pine Bluff Arsenal in Arkansas. These trailers were found to contain hundreds of illegal weapons, ammunition, explosives and other ordinance hidden in, supposedly empty, army containers. Transported and reported as empty, these containers had been returned from Vietnam to the arsenals in Milan and Pine Bluff for reuse. It is speculated that these containers were not empty when returned, and had been transferred to Maxwell Trucking trailers for sale and distribution to illegal markets. These illegal markets were reported to be controlled by a group of underworld figures – known as the Memphis Mafia. Major arrests included Steve Carrollton – reported leader of the Memphis Mafia – General Sandy Samson of the Milan Arsenal and General Darrell Taylor of the Pine Bluff Arsenal. Also arrested were the COO and President of Wayne Knitting Hosiery Mill, Gerald Wayne. The President and owner of Maxwell Trucking, JR Maxwell had died mysteriously earlier this week, and it is suspected his death was related to these activities. Numerous other arrests of drivers, dock personnel, army warehouse managers and other management of Maxwell Trucking were underway, and should continue throughout the day and into the weekend as the investigations continue.

~

I went quickly the phone and called Jack. Unbelievably he was in his office.

"Jack, I've got a friend who is mixed up in this Humboldt mess, but I know she is innocent," I said anxiously.

"She?" Jack asked.

"Yes she. Her name is Judy Strong and she is/was the Executive Vice President Sales for Maxwell Trucking."

"Wow. With JR Maxwell dead, she is in the gun sights of the FBI, you can count on that."

"I know. I expect to talk with her later today, and I will have her call you at first opportunity. Meanwhile, grab your luggage and get up here, she needs your help and I need you to help her."

"Is your head, your heart or some other part of your body making these decisions?" Jack asked.

"It's my head.  She is innocent, and they will crucify her without some quality legal help."

"You're sure she is innocent?" he didn't seem convinced.

"Yes, I am absolutely sure."

"Okay, I'll be there as soon as I can.  Have her call me; she must give me authority to speak as her attorney.  Without that, I can't do much."

"Done, I'll see you later," I said hurriedly.

~

Judy finally called about 2:00, and she had been arrested.  But she was at the County jail, not in Jackson.  Silly her, she had used her one phone call on me.  I told her my plan and assured her that Jack could and would take care of her.  Then I asked if Scotty was close.  He was, and I had her give him the phone.

"Scotty, this girl needs to make another call.  She now has the number of her lawyer in Memphis and must contact him.  She didn't have the number and called me to get it – okay?"

"No problem.  We'll make it happen," Scotty assured.

~

Just when the crowd started to gather and just before Nickie exploded, Leroy finally showed up.

"Thank goodness. I thought there was going to be a riot if you didn't show up soon. Without that stupid jukebox, this crowd had the attitude of a lynch mob."

"Remember Carson, you can't change their habits. They are not a wine and cheese group!" Leroy laughed.

"Let's get out of here. We need to talk," I said headed to the door.

As I discussed my plan, Leroy drove me to Deloch Auto Repair to get my car. When he left me there, he was heading to the Maxwell house to visit with Mary Ellen and Liz. They would discuss the details of my plan and put the wheels in motion to hopefully bring this case to a close tomorrow.

My plan depended upon a lie that should bring out the truth. I was counting on particular personality flaws that I felt were vulnerable. The lie had to be convincing or it wouldn't work, but I had to trust my faith in people's view of their own self. What they see in the mirror is rarely what others see.

~

With the Ford back on the highway, I felt like a free man again. I drove back to Chiefs, parked at Cottage 4 and wandered into the bar to finish the evening. My 'Out of Order' sign was now pasted across the front of the TV screen, and my corner office was occupied by three lovely ladies and four guys, who had probably just parked their tractor outside!

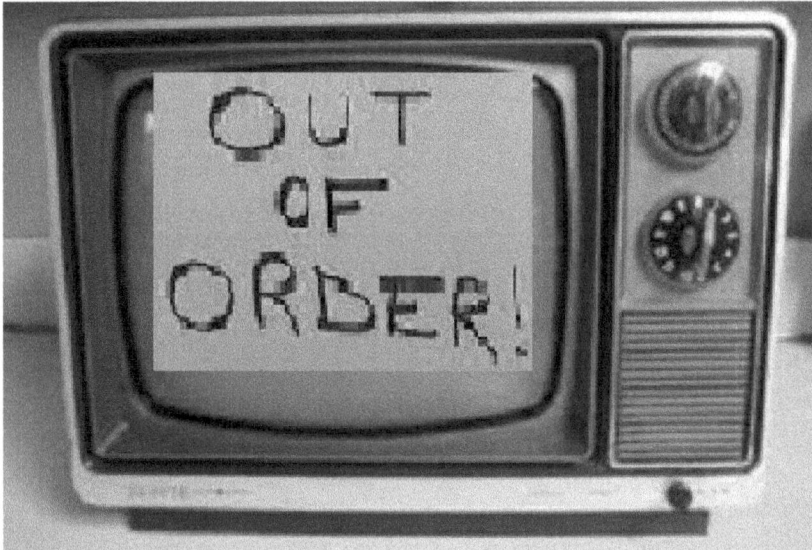

I found a seat at the end of Nickie's bar, and she kept me watered with Jack/Coke until I just couldn't handle that jukebox anymore.

After making a quick call to Leroy to confirm our plans were in place, I was off to bed in Cottage 4. I expected to be sleeping in my own bed tomorrow night.

# DAY TEN
# FINAL DAY

# Final Day

The day started early for everyone.

Figuring it was still too early for Dorothy to be awake; Leroy placed a call to the Wayne house at about 8:30 AM. Today was Saturday and Carrie Mae's day off. After 10 or 12 rings there was still no answer, but we knew she was home. On the third try Dorothy finally answered her phone. It was obvious, and painful to the listener, that she was suffering from a serious hangover; however, that was not unusual for her.

"Yes, Leroy, how can I help you? Isn't it awful early for you to be calling your citizens?" Her words came out hard.

"Yes, and I apologize for the hour, but I have some difficult news to deliver," Leroy started. "The FBI has released your husband. However, my office has now arrested him again for the murder of JR Maxwell. I am holding him in my jail and I need you to come down, speak with him and bring him a few personal items. Can you do that this morning?"

"What? Arrested? Murder of JR Maxwell?" she was speaking from her foggy mind. "Are you crazy? Lester Blankenship is the killer, and you have him in your jail already. I don't understand?"

"Dorothy, I really can't discuss details over the phone. His sister, Mary Ellen Maxwell has provided an alibi for Lester and we have other evidence linking Gerald to the murder. I will be happy to discuss this with you when you get down to the office."

She never really hung up the phone. She threw it in anger or just dropped it, either way the connection remained until Leroy hung up on his end.

Dorothy also never dressed and, amazingly, didn't grab the vodka. What she did do was storm out of the house, get in her red Thunderbird and streak out of the long Wayne driveway.

I have heard that women in pajamas and housecoats drive faster than those dressed normally. I'm not sure about that, but the normal 10-minute trip from her house to the Maxwell home took her less than 5 minutes. Leroy had a deputy discreetly following, just to make sure there were no detours. She followed the plan perfectly.

After making the sharp turn into the Maxwell driveway, Dorothy never stopped the car before opening the door and getting out. The Thunderbird remained in gear and came to rest against some tall shrubs, just a few feet from the house main entrance. This lady was very upset!

The Maxwell home main entrance opened into an open hallway, with a formal dining and living room to the left. Immediately to the right was a slightly sunken den with fireplace, wet-bar and large windows overlooking the pool area. An adjoining closed hallway, past the dining area, lead to the split-level where bedrooms and baths were located. The kitchen was partially hidden and off to the rear of the den. Leroy and I were waiting and watching from the kitchen area.

Dorothy was standing in her pajamas and furiously pounding on the front door. When Mary Ellen finally opened it, Dorothy pushed the door, and her, – hard – back into a planter near the living area. "Mary Ellen, you bitch," she screamed. "What do you think you are doing? Telling lies about my husband and telling lies to give an alibi for Lester!"

"Dorothy, what are you talking about? What's wrong with you?" Mary Ellen replied as she got up from the floor and began slowly moving down into the den, hoping to avoid another attack.

"I'm talking about the police arresting my husband for the murder of your husband, that's what I'm talking about!" she yelled.

"Dorothy, they have evidence that he committed the murder," Mary Ellen answered while still slowly moving toward the den area.

"What evidence?" Dorothy screamed.

"His car was seen at the Tennessee Motel at the time of the murder, and they have his fingerprints on the gun."

"His car? Why has no one told me about his car? Fingerprints? There were no fingerprints on the gun," Dorothy was still yelling.

"How do you know that?" Mary Ellen asked having successfully made her way to the sunken den.

"Because, well, I read it in the news," Dorothy stuttered.

"No you didn't. There has never been any mention of fingerprints in the news or by the police."

"I don't care, he didn't do it. Lester did it. I know he did." Dorothy continued to yell and follow Mary Ellen into the den.

"How do you know that Dorothy?" Mary Ellen asked as she finally stopped moving and stood up straight to face Dorothy.

"I just do. And how can you provide an alibi for someone who killed your husband? Are you as crazy as that half-brother and your cheating husband?" Dorothy laughed.

"My husband is gone and I can't bring him back," Mary Ellen said firmly. "But I can save the only sibling I have. If you hadn't been jerking his pants down at every opportunity, I might have been able to keep him out of the trouble he is in now. Dimwit or not, he is still my brother."

Dorothy was calming, but her anger was getting deeper and deeper. Her bloodshot eyes were showing the rage that had been growing in her for many years.

"Don't you mean half-brother and half wit? He's so stupid he probably thinks he did kill JR," she said with a cruel laugh while staring hard at Mary Ellen.

"I thought you just said that he did kill JR?" Mary Ellen countered.

"Well, he did, and Gerald didn't," Dorothy stuttered. "I know that." She was frustrated.

"What about the car? What about the fingerprints?"

"I don't know," Dorothy said while inching closer to where Mary Ellen was standing. "Maybe Lester stole the car; maybe he borrowed the car, maybe anything. But I do know one thing. Years ago you took the man I loved from me, and then left me broken and embarrassed in a two bit town in Arkansas. Now that I've found someone who loves and cares for me, you are going to lie for a dimwitted half-brother and take that man away too. I won't let it happen." She was still inching closer to Mary Ellen.

"Dorothy, what about his fingerprints on the gun?" Mary Ellen asked desperately.

"Damn it, Mary Ellen, I told you there were no fingerprints," she screamed. "I wiped that gun clean, so I know there is no way my husband's prints could be on that gun!"

Mary Ellen was silent.

When Dorothy realized what she had said, she had no choice but to continue. "Yes bitch, I shot him," she sneered. "I shot him while he was pleading with me not to do it. But it felt good, it made up for all the hurt that bastard had given me for all these many years. You, and your fancy dress, your fancy words and your fancy friends - you stole him from me, and now I stole him from you! He's dead and I'm glad." Dorothy was only a few feet from Mary Ellen when she spoke.

Mary Ellen was losing it. "Oh my!" she said in shock.

"Yes, and I just might as well send you to join him," Dorothy said before lunging at Mary Ellen. Dorothy's hands were on Mary Ellen's throat and they both fell onto the couch before rolling onto the floor.

Leroy grabbed Dorothy within seconds. He had her handcuffed before I could get Mary Ellen back on the couch.

Dorothy screamed, "You tricked me, you bastards! You bastards tricked me!"

I looked at her and said, "Yes my dear – we did."

Leroy and his deputy walked Dorothy out the front door and put her in the cruiser. She was still screaming, struggling, cursing and crying – the jail was going to have a new and interesting guest.

When things settled, I sat down with Mary Ellen and Liz at the kitchen table.

"I know that was tough, Mary Ellen," I said to them both.

"Yes, but thank you for talking me into doing it," Mary Ellen said wiping away tears. "This way I have some comfort in JR's death - knowing the truth."

I continued. "She played Lester all along. He faked the break-in here at the house, and then provided a false tip to get me back to Humboldt. At some point, probably during my last visit here, he stole the gun from my glove box and then their plan was set. I'm certain Dorothy was pulling his strings and telling him what to do, but probably when it came down to actually shooting JR – he balked. However, Dorothy had no apprehension about pulling the trigger, and as you heard her say, she actually enjoyed it. Selfish people do selfish things and are only concerned with themselves – usually with total disregard for others. Dorothy fits that mold. That is the reason I thought this plan might work, and it did."

Liz spoke, "Well, whatever has happened is over. We all need to move on."

"Well spoken, and that is just exactly what I intend to do," I said getting up from the table. "I've got a couple of stops to make and then point my wounded car toward Memphis."

"You know, Carson, you and I never did have that breakfast you promised." Liz was teasing me again.

"Tell you what," I grinned. "You call me the next time you get off that big airplane in Memphis. I'll promise you the largest breakfast Peabody Hotel has to offer. A deal?"

"That is a deal!" Liz said smiling.

I got a hug from both Mary Ellen and Liz, plus a little extra ear nibble from Liz. Guess we might be having breakfast sooner than I thought!

I stopped at Chiefs to grab my things and tell Nickie and Ronnie good-by.

"Handsome, it has been fun and exciting," Nickie said as I was paying my bill. "When will we see you again?"

Walking out the front door I yelled back, "Soon I hope, but certainly before that jukebox runs out of songs to play. Love you both, talk with you next trip."

~

My next stop was the sheriff's office, which was on my way out of town. Jack and Judy were sitting behind the glass in an interview room. I watched for a few minutes, and I'm not sure they could get any legal work done for smiling at each other. This was probably going to be a good lawyer client relationship, in more ways than one!

I tapped on the glass and Judy ran out.

"Oh, Carson, thank you so much for your help," she was ecstatic. "Jack has gotten it all figured out, and maybe I can help Mary Ellen save what is left of Maxwell Trucking. And guess what else?"

"What?"

"I won't go to jail!" Judy exclaimed.

"Honey, that is the way it was planned," I said with confidence. "I'll leave you in Jack's very capable hands, because I need to get back to Memphis; there are other clients who need my attention."

I got another hug, and this time, a big kiss from Judy. She went back into the interview room and I waved good-bye to Jack. He knew we would talk later.

~

I glanced at my watch as I pulled out onto Hwy 79 headed home. I had the windows down allowing the fresh air to blow away all the bad memory of the past several days. However, I had made some friendships that would probably prove to be good for Carson Reno in the future.

The jazz music soothed my tied mind, and if I didn't make any stops and cheated the speed limit - I could probably still make the 'tea dance' with Rita at *'The Starlight'* Lounge.

# Photo Credits

classic-car-history.com

photo.net

fwix.com

Poynter.org

flickr.com

desktopcar.net

vinothkumarm.blogspot.com

artfreelancer.com

radaris.com

nicenfunnys.blogspot.com

hi-spec-eng.com

bradfordvotech.com

theopiumgroup.com

oceandrivemiamibeach.com

memphisite.com

library.uthsc.edu

elvisweek.com

terragalleria.com

harahanbridge.com

laborphotos.cornell.edu

# About the Author

A Florida native, Gerald grew up in the small town of Humboldt, TN. He attended high school and was a graduate of HHS class of 64. Following graduation from the Univ. of Tenn, he spent time in Hopkinsville, KY, Memphis, TN and Newport, AR before moving back to Florida – where he now lives.

This short story is fictional. *Murder in Humboldt* is what the author calls 'Fiction for Fun'. It uses real places and real geography to spin a story that didn't happen, but should be fun for the mystery reader. A quick read, those familiar with the 1962 geography in the novel, will travel back in time to places that will be always remembered.

His first book, Don't Wake Me Until It's Time to Go, is a collection of stories, events and humorous observations from his life. As a non-fiction book, many friends and readers will find themselves in one of his adventures or stories.

**Learn more about this author and his additional works at:**

http://wix.com/carsonreno/carson

http://www.authorsden.com/geraldwdarnell

**and**

http://stores.lulu.com/geralddarnell

**When visiting the web-sites, you are encouraged to leave your comments and reviews of this book and his others.**

**Also, please let the author know if you would like to see continuing stories with Carson Reno and his cast of characters.**

**Be sure to watch for Carson's next adventure – "The Price of Beauty in Strawberry Land."**

# "Life is Cheap – Make Sure You Buy Enough"

## Carson Reno

Lightning Source UK Ltd.
Milton Keynes UK
UKHW011509080822
407006UK00002B/465

9 780557 734160